LUCIFER

Fire From Heaven - Book 1

AVA MARTELL

GET IN TOUCH

Sign up for Ava Martell's newsletter to receive updates on new releases as well as free sneak previews of what's coming next in the Fire From Heaven series.

Follow Ava on social media

Facebook
Twitter
Tumblr
Instagram

Official site
avamartell.com

For my mother

I

LUCIFER

I am called many things.

Prince of Lies. Lord of Hell. The Supreme Tempter of Mankind. Once, years beyond counting ago, I was the Bringer of Light. The Morningstar. *His* favorite.

And now? I'm all those things and much much more, but I stick with Lucifer.

It just rolls off the tongue, doesn't it? The screamers always emphasize the first syllable, drawing the rest out in a shriek or a gurgle, depending on if I'm in the mood for quiet torment that day.

The criers, they irritate me most of all. They choke the letters down like a child swallowing bitter medicine while they stare up at me with pleading eyes, hoping to be the one that incites the Devil to mercy.

The broken ones have silent, dead eyes ignoring the torturers and demons that surround them. Sometimes I'll hear my name on their breath, a barely audible wheeze as they resign themselves to Hell.

I can hear the disgust. What did you expect? Hearts and sunshine? I'm the *Devil*.

Or I was. On Earth, I'm beginning to feel like I'm something else entirely. Something new.

Nothing has been new for a very long time.

Every generation of humanity seems to think that they've reinvented it all. The most efficient ways to murder each other. The most depraved sexual acts.

Please.

After eons of violence and sex, I can assure humanity that everything is a remix. Everything has been done before.

I do admit though, that the 21st century has perfected it to a fine art. The children are raised on video games that mimic violence flawlessly, racking up body counts that my top lieutenants would envy before they're old enough to drive.

And then there's the internet. Every flavor of pornography from the mundane to the type that can make the Devil wince is ripe for the viewing from the privacy of your own home.

I wonder if my Father is impressed with what His beloved creations have made of this world.

I tempt, but I don't put ideas or desires into any mortal's head. All I've ever done is silence that little voice that says *shouldn't can't wrong*. I just bring those visceral wants and needs you bury deep inside to the surface.

I never handed humanity the rope, I just stood in the background and watched as you tied it into a noose and strangled the world.

That's all the past.

Even your favorite pastime will grow tedious when you count time in millennia.

The Devil is bored, but that's not what leads me to contemplate ripping my way out of this dungeon of my own creation.

Enrollment is down.

Since the beginning of it all, a steady stream of souls has

poured through Hell, an unending tide of broken humanity flooding the pits with their wretched fate. As time passed and the millennium came and went, the numbers increased to a veritable tsunami of souls, ripe with sin and ready for the plucking.

Until now.

It would be easy to blame the sudden drought on the humans themselves but the likelihood of the populace suddenly finding a religion other than the unholy trinity of sex, power and money was slim at best.

No, I know exactly who is responsible for the sudden drought in Hell.

The Archangels. I've always been a gambling man, but this hardly even counts as a wager.

Michael is behind this.

I gaze across the cold, blackness of Hell. My domain. My creation. Everything I am, and all I have left.

And Michael is trying to rip it away from me.

All things being said, the balance of souls that end up falling in my grasp and *His* most favored lambs that skip their way into Heaven's embrace has always been just that – a balance. That balance was tipping in my favor until now.

Calling human souls mere *currency* is insultingly inadequate. A soul isn't a thing that can be bought or sold. It can't be traded like livestock. In its purest form, a human soul is power. Souls aren't the fruit on the vine. They are the soil and the oxygen, the very sunlight that feeds the tree.

Or they are until the reach my realm.

Damming that tide of souls might prevent them from crossing my threshold, but it certainly can't keep the wicked from expiring, and even the pleasure of spiting me wouldn't be enough to entice Michael to taint Heaven with those souls. That leaves only one place.

Barred from Hell and unwanted in Heaven, they are

caught on Earth. The havoc hasn't begun yet, but I can already feel it brewing on the surface.

The souls of the damned will poison Earth as surely as chemical runoff, but Michael and his cohorts will consider it a worthwhile sacrifice to weaken Hell.

I don't.

That's where the stories always get it wrong. I punish evil. I don't create it. In my impulsive youth, I might have relished in watching Pestilence and Famine ride through villages, spreading disease and starvation with the ease of a tree dropping pollen. Once, I carried my own bloody sword beside War and laughed as Death trailed us on that infernal pale horse.

"Come and see," I would whisper, and they would follow me like beasts to the slaughter.

But they were never innocents. I couldn't claim a truly pure soul if I wanted to, but why would I bother when untold millions were begging for a place in my kingdom. Seventy-two virgins aren't nearly as amusing as one painted whore.

And where better to find amusement than among the throngs of humanity?

A walk in the world would solve my little boredom issue quite nicely, and if I have the chance to tear Michael's wings off. . . Well, that would just be a nice bonus to my vacation.

LEAVING Hell isn't quite as simple as strolling out the exit door, even for me. It was made to be a cage to punish the wicked and the Fallen, myself especially.

When I fell from Heaven, light surrounded me. I was the Morningstar, after all. The cold, pale glow of Heaven grew brighter around me as I plummeted to Earth, searing my skin and burning my wings black.

It was my last memory of pain, at least my own, until now.

Leaving Hell is much more of a crawl. Serpentine tunnels wind through the depths, dug by demons and broken souls over the millennia. Only the highest ranking in Hell know where they lead, and even fewer could find their way to the gates.

The tunnels are the deepest of black. No torches light the way, no errant embers of brimstone illuminate the path. The darkness is thick. It oozes over my flesh like tar, swallowing the remnants of light filtering in from the tunnel's mouth. My shoulders brush the walls of the narrow pathway, and rough stone sticky with unknown moisture plucks at the feathers of my wings.

The walls grow tighter and the rough stone gives way to jagged shards that cut into a body that has been whole for millennia, and I know pain.

Demons may have carved the tunnels themselves, but these last few feet before the gates were wrought by the divine.

This is going to hurt.

I push forward, every cell in my body rebelling against the long forgotten touch of divinity, and—

The tunnel widens into a room with a single door appearing to rest against bare stone. The rough-hewn wood is unadorned. *He* never did have much of a flair for dramatics. The slightest bit of illumination escapes from the cracks around the edges, that tiny bit of light cutting through the blackness.

I hesitate. The full force of what I'm about to do presses against me.

For one brief moment, I consider turning back, but I've never exactly been one who considered the long-term outcomes of my choices.

Fuck it, I think and push open the door.

I AWAKE ON A BEACH. Sprawled on my back on the damp sand, the low tide waves lapping against my body soak my clothes, and I stare upward at the sky. Clear, achingly bright blue hiding the Heaven I've forsaken. The doorway to the Hell I've abandoned vanished when I stepped across the threshold.

I'm here.

Earth.

I can feel the mass of humanity all around. Buzzing in my ears like a swarm of insects are countless hidden thoughts and a million whispered sins.

I sit up slowly, shaking off the last vestiges of pain as my tattered skin knits itself back together. I cast my eyes around my surroundings, pondering where precisely the portal has dumped me out.

Not that it matters. I can cross continents in no time at all, the span of my wings tearing through the miles, but never let it be said that the Devil isn't curious.

The beach is deserted. No mortals witness the sudden appearance of a winged man on a Tuesday morning. Almost as an afterthought, I will my wings away, tucking them into invisibility. If I want to lose myself in the surge of humankind, that is the first step.

I take another, my toes sinking into the sand. A torn flyer sticks up from the sand near my feet, the half-buried neon green paper screaming up from the ground. I grab it, brushing the dust off the crumpled paper to find an ad for $2 Hurricanes on Bourbon Street.

New Orleans then.

My lips curl into a smile.

This is going to be fun.

2

GRACE

New Orleans.

Every lost soul seems to end up here eventually. I'm no different.

Someone with a better option generally isn't warming a barstool at 2 o'clock on Tuesday. I stare down the gleaming mahogany bar, remnants of a different age, before turning back to the swirling amber contents of my glass. I knock back the watery dregs of my whiskey, relishing the burn before signaling the bartender for another.

Go to college, they said. *You're nothing without a degree.*

You like to write? Be a journalist. That's a respected field.

I snort at the thought. Maybe a decade ago I would have waltzed out of grad school and into an internship. From there, a paid gig and I'd be staring at my byline from those wrinkled pages for the rest of my career.

Not anymore.

More papers close up shop every day, and the magazines are following suit. Bloggers rule the news world now, and in the cutthroat realm of the internet, you're dead in the water unless you have an angle that brings in the clicks.

Right now my only angle is my desperate desire to pay the overdue student loan bill buried in the bottom of my purse.

The bartender returns with a new glass, filled to the brim with the harsh well whiskey. It tastes like paint thinner that dreams of being whiskey when it grows up, but even that manages to be a splurge for me right now.

"I made it a double," the bartender says, setting the glass down in front of me. "No charge. You look like you need it."

A few years ago, I would have bristled at the assumption that I *needed* anything, but now I just smile gratefully and sip my drink, the smoky flavor letting me forget just for awhile.

I'm not another tourist or a person who moved here on a whim after too many Anne Rice novels. I grew up here, eating beignets with my parents as a child and coating my face with powdered sugar.

"Looks like we're getting some snow this year, Gracie!" The terrible dad jokes rolled so easily off my father's tongue as he ruffled my blonde curls, brushing away the sugar that had landed there while my mother sipped a cafe au lait and giggled at his antics.

We were so happy then.

I'd learned to drive on those narrow, twisting streets, weaving my dad's battered red Jeep down Magazine Street at 16, white knuckling it at the endless stream of tourists and locals that seemed to ignore every traffic rule my parents had been drilling into my young mind.

I hadn't been driving that day.

I take another sip of whiskey, trying to dampen the memories that threaten to bubble up. The scent of scorched rubber and hot metal. The glint of the red and blue lights making the shards of glass littering the street sparkle in the night. The sharp, metallic taste of blood on my lips and the bracing scent of ozone in the air.

Coming back here was a mistake.

I loved this city with a fierce devotion usually only reserved for a soulmate or a beloved family member. I thought seven years was enough time to numb my loss to the point that I could start over in the only place I'd ever considered *home*.

Turns out my major wasn't the only thing I was wrong about.

After the accident, I was shipped off to my father's sister. Kind but far from nurturing, Aunt Caroline was a big shot divorce lawyer in Boston. She and her husband had never wanted kids, so being thrust into the guardianship of an emotionally destroyed teenager was an adjustment for everyone.

Understatement of the century there.

Spending the first 16 years of my life in New Orleans where the wild, vibrant energy of the city permeates your surroundings as inevitably as the humidity didn't begin to prepare me for Boston.

The narrow, confusing streets made to fit carriages rather than SUVs were familiar, but beyond that, I might as well have been on another planet. The sky was a uniform shade of dull grey when I touched down on the runway, dragging my mother's worn leather suitcase behind me.

I stepped out of the airport, barely hearing my Aunt's words about school and sending for the rest of my things. I followed behind her, the dull thump of my boots on the damp asphalt filling my ears instead.

I remember the cold most of all. In the rush to bring me to the safety of adult supervision and settle me into my new life, no one had considered that I didn't own anything warmer than a hoodie. October in Boston was a very different beast than back home, and I spent that first day quivering like a leaf until my Aunt noticed and handed me a pile of

Harvard sweatshirts to bury myself in until we could go shopping for something appropriate.

I sigh, dropping my empty whiskey glass onto the bar with a faint clunk. The last thing I intended to do was spend my day dredging up old ghosts, but that's the thing with New Orleans.

Ghosts are everywhere here. It doesn't matter if you believe in the supernatural or not, after a few weeks in this city it crawls inside you. You never even notice the transition from comfortable skepticism until you find yourself popping into a voodoo shop to pick up a gris-gris bag before a first date and the cleansing you use your Florida water for has nothing to do with making your floors shine.

My ghosts are nowhere more present than right at home. Aunt Caroline had enough forethought to know that I'd end up back on the cracked doorstep of my parents' house one day. She managed to find a few student renters over the last seven years, charging exorbitant deposits and cheap rent to attract someone more likely to love the house than destroy it.

The most recent was a nursing student at Tulane who had vacated the place for a job in Chicago after graduation. Suddenly, my home was mine again.

It seemed as good a sign as any that it was a time to come back.

Unlocking the yellow door of that shotgun house after so many years. . . it still takes my breath away. I push the door shut behind me, closing out the noise and the bustle of uptown and walk into the silent house.

The world seems muffled in here. The house was always rented furnished, so the years barely changed it. The deep crimson of the living room that my mother had insisted on in a fit of gothic fancy when I was ten still makes the room a bit too dark.

Standing like sentinels in each corner of the room are

the four straight-backed "company chairs" upholstered in cream velvet. I've never once seen anyone sit on those uncomfortable chairs, but Mom had dragged them home from a shuttering antique shop one day, and there they had stayed.

My old bedroom was relegated to a storage closet by most of the tenants. The pulpy horror novels I favored at that age still line the bookshelves, and the narrow twin bed is hidden under a bold green and blue tapestry I've never seen before, no doubt abandoned by another college senior who outgrew a freshman year hippie aesthetic.

Across the hall, the door to the larger bedroom is shut, heavy oak keeping it locked in the past for just a few more minutes. I grasp the brass knob, the finish having long since been worn down to a dull gold and turn it a bit harder than necessary.

It's so bare. The queen-sized bed dominates the center of the room, and the massive mahogany wardrobe and dresser take up another wall. The various knick-knacks and tangled mess of necklaces that covered that surface are still locked in storage with the rest of the personal items.

After so much time it's impossible, but I would swear on a stack of Bibles that I can still smell her perfume lingering in the air, lush rose with just the slightest hint of jasmine.

A perfect mirror of when I left, I returned to New Orleans with only what I could stuff in my mother's old suitcase. Funny how even now I can't let myself claim any of it as mine. My mother's suitcase. My parents' house. Even when I look in the mirror, all I can see is the mix of the two of them that somehow created me.

I've long since stopped talking about my loss to anyone. After seven years, everyone expects you to have moved on. Aunt Caroline still gets a bit misty-eyed on Dad's birthday, but beyond that, she has her own life to live. Other than a sadly wistful smile when anyone mentions his name, she's fine.

I lost touch with most of my New Orleans friends in the tumultuous first year in Boston. I don't blame any of them for it. After too many stilted phone conversations where I broke down in tears railing at the unfairness of life and how much I hated Boston and the universe for stealing my parents and my Aunt for daring to be alive, the calls stopped coming.

Long emails turned into cursory messages about their lives, filled with bright snapshots of parades and festivals, and eventually, those were traded in for Facebook updates. Likes and one sentence comments were all I had left of my childhood friends.

As for Boston, I'd been shoved into a tiny private school by my Aunt's office halfway through my junior year. The children of the Boston elite hadn't known quite what to make of me with my bright clothes and slow Louisiana drawl. Even locked in grief, my open Southern attitude didn't fit with the standoffish New Englanders, so any friendships slid over the surface of my life like an oil slick, never penetrating who I really was.

Leaving had been an easy choice, but returning to New Orleans wasn't.

Somehow I expected myself to fit back into my old life. I was supposed to unlock my front door and be welcomed back home, instantly falling into a job and friendships. Maybe even a relationship. My life here should have just been on pause, waiting for me to come back and take up my rightful place again.

Instead, the city moved on without me. I'm lucky enough that the house has long since been paid off, but my loans are coming due, and a paid in full mortgage doesn't cover utilities.

My parent's modest life insurance policies were enough to

buy me a car and cover my books and expenses at school, but beyond that, I'm on my own now. With too much pride to call my Aunt begging for money, I took the first job I could find, slinging shots at one of the many forgettable bars lining Bourbon Street.

Inside the bar, I'm not a sad, lonely orphan hiding from her own memories anymore. Once I pull on the skimpy black tank top with SPIRITS scrawled across my breasts, I can be someone else. Someone who flirts with tourists, catching the gaze of over-served college students and luring them to buy yet another round of shots because everything tastes better out of a blinking plastic skull.

The party never stops on Bourbon Street, and the moment I cross the threshold of that bar each night, I make those words my life philosophy.

Inside the bar, my coworkers call me G, and being that girl is so much easier. For a few hours each night, I can forget about being Grace with her solitude and overdue bills. Even more, I can forget the shadow of Gracie, the girl frozen in time with her smile and her happy family.

Compartmentalizing my life to that degree might be a few county lines over from "healthy," but I'd spent too many years taking the advice of everyone in my life who considered themselves older and wiser. All that got me was a useless degree and whole lot of sadness.

Now my therapy is painting my lips hot pink and pasting a wide smile across them while I pour glass after glass of sticky sweet booze for minimum wage and whatever extra dollars I can entice a Spring Breaker to shove inside the glitter encrusted plastic skull we use as a tip jar. Maybe if I laugh loud enough and smile big enough I can lose myself in the bright lights of the city and finally forget.

❦ 3 ❦

LUCIFER

S o this is the world.

Honestly, I expected more.

New Orleans. The utter epicenter of debauchery and excess. A town that built a large chunk of its economy on binge drinking and public nudity. If I can't manage to find a diversion here, I'm out of luck.

Noticing any effects my stolen souls might be having on the populace though? That will be another matter entirely. A normal day in this city resembles a Roman orgy, so witnessing the outcome of Michael's plot won't be easy here.

"Lucifer."

I stop, the shock at hearing my name on the lips of a human causing me to freeze in the crowded sidewalk. A mortal would have found himself jostled by irritated travelers intent on reaching the bottom of another glass as soon as possible. Instead, they flow around me like an oblivious school of fish, some instinctual lizard brain warning them away from getting too close.

Except for this one.

She is old. Her white hair twists into a tight rope that

coils around her head like a snake readying itself to strike. Deep wrinkles are etched into the coffee-colored skin of her face, and her clothing hangs in a riot of color around her. A small chalkboard sign with "Palm Reading $20" scrawled across it in thin, spiderweb handwriting dangles carelessly from one of her gnarled hands.

"Come to read my palm then?"

She takes a step closer, and I smell the thick scent of incense wafting from her clothes with each step. I cock my head to the side, trying to figure out this creature's game.

There have always been mortals who can sense the divine and the demonic. But these days they aren't usually quite so overt. The old woman stops and stands her ground when scarcely a foot separates us from each other. "You aren't supposed to be here," she states, her low voice scolding me like I am a naughty child.

"Really?" I drawl. "And why is that?"

"You know why. I can see those black wings trailing behind you. They won't save you here."

I throw my head back and laugh, the sound making the crowd around me falter in their steps for just a moment. Abruptly my amusement ceases. "What makes you think I'm the one who needs saving?" I hiss.

Of all the replies that I might expect, I don't anticipate her grasping my hand and yanking me closer.

"He's coming for her. And you aren't strong enough to stop him. He'll tear you apart, one feather at a time if you get in his way. And you'll get in his way." She clutches my hand with an impossible strength that belies her small, frail body. Her dark eyes flash as they gaze into mine before releasing my hand and melting back into the crowd.

I whirl around, my eyes scanning the street for her, but the old woman has disappeared into the sea of people, leaving me with nothing but her warning and the feeling of her papery flesh against my palm.

Curiouser and curiouser.

Who is she? The old woman intrigues me, but she is far from the first witch or medium I've ever run across in the centuries. Generally, those of her kind that end up on my doorstep are more interested in clamoring for a spot in Hell's court than offering up cryptic warnings.

I chuckle softly, the idea that I could be in any danger amusing in its ludicrousness. Short of a pack of Archangels or my Father, nothing on this plain of existence can touch me.

Michael and his cohorts are on Earth. There is no doubt about that anymore. Only an Archangel or four will have the raw power needed to trap souls that want nothing more than to move on. And only the Archangels are callous enough to rip apart His beloved world just to irritate me.

Since the beginning, we all disdained the sweaty, greedy bunch that my Father so adored. I was simply the only one with big enough stones to mention my disgust in my Father's presence. The others laughed at humanity, savoring the weakness and pain of the bald monkeys that played at having power and grumbled at any mission that sent them down into the muck of the world.

Short of raising the four horsemen and tearing a bloody swath across the Mississippi, they won't care what I do to this planet.

As for dear old Dad, He turned his back on us all long ago. Good or otherwise, he walked away and left us all to our own devices. The angels abandoned humanity, and in their absence, they turned to me and mine.

And after a few thousand years, the bald monkeys grow on you.

I duck into a bar, eager for a respite, however brief, from the crush of souls outside as I plot my next move. In a city where $200 will buy your own personal parade, a quiet moment to think becomes even more valuable.

The cool darkness of the bar slips over me with comforting familiarity, blotting out the mid-afternoon hedonism outside the thick wooden door. I sink down into one of the worn leather barstools and catch a glimpse of my face in the mirrored wall, seeing myself as they see me for the first time.

I look weary.

A casual observer will see nothing more than a tall man in a well-cut suit, a bit too dark to be practical in the Louisiana heat. If they draw a bit closer, they might find a different sort of heat burning in them, enticing them to take that last step and meet my eyes, letting every secret spill from their lips and their souls as their needy human flesh begs for just one touch.

Never let it be said that the Devil neglects aesthetics.

To my own eyes though, I can see the weight of the years upon me. Hell is so much more simple for the other Fallen. The angels that follow me so eagerly crave nothing more than another leader they can follow with blind obedience. The humans that find their way to my realm for punishment are all too quick to shed their mortal coil and replace it with a demonic skin if it gives them the chance to become the torturer instead of the one strapped to the rack.

There are always holdouts. Free will, after all. My Father bestowed that gift on his humans, and even the most rank will try to resist the call of their true nature at first, but Hell is, above all, repetition. The knowledge that at the end of each day they become whole and the cycle begins anew snaps them all eventually. They forget their lives and crimes. Even their very names fade into nothingness.

That's how demons are born. Every demon slithering through Hell or tormenting someone topside was just another person once upon a time. Bit by bit, Hell scrapes away their free will along with their humanity.

Why my Father gave me free will, I expect I'll never know. No doubt it was just another ingredient my Father threw into creation for his own divine amusement.

The bartender leans against the back of the bar, watching me expectantly from her spot next to the gin selection.

"Whiskey. Something smoky to remind me of home. And leave the bottle."

At the order she scrambles to grab a bottle from the top shelf, filling a rocks glass with two fingers of the amber liquid before backing off and leaving the dusty bottle beside me.

I take a sip, letting the taste of burnt sugar and dark oak flow over my tongue, but the taste I truly savor comes from the sins of the pretty red-haired bartender. Her fingers just brush mine as she hands me the glass, and almost unconsciously my mind ticks off the seven deadlies she breaks on the regular.

Greed. Her quick fingers pocket whatever cash might not be missed from the register.

Wrath. Shattering the headlights on an ex-boyfriend's car.

Lust. So much lust. Tugging up her tank top to flash those milky breasts after a few too many shots. Dragging a handsy blond man for a quickie in the supply room mid-shift. Leering at a dark-haired stripper exiting the Penthouse Club.

And the heat in her eyes as she stares at me.

One word. One *thought*, and I could have her on her pretty pale knees in the middle of this bar. I certainly didn't come back to the world to live as a penitent, and lust always was such a fun sin.

She licks her lips unconsciously as she watches me, every molecule of her body screaming for me to take her and ruin her for the touch of mortal men.

It was just too easy.

I turn my attention back to my drink, feeling a spark of anger from her at the dismissal, but the redhead is forgotten before I swallow my next sip.

"He's coming for her."

The old witch's words bounce through my mind.

"He's coming for her. And you aren't strong enough to stop him. He'll tear you apart, one feather at a time if you get in his way. And you'll get in his way."

I know prophecy when I hear it. The vague riddles of prophets have always done little more than irritate me. Who is she? And more importantly, why would I care about the fate of one human above the rest?

❧ 4 ❧

GRACE

Someone is following me.

Just because New Orleans never sleeps doesn't mean every street is packed like Mardi Gras 24/7. In the small hours of the morning between when the drinkers stumble back to their hotels and the lucky bartenders and shot girls count their tips at home, the streets empty. Anyone still out has a reason.

Mine was pure bad luck. Two of the three frozen daiquiri machines died mid-shift forcing us to use the remaining one until it was practically smoking. As the new girl, I drew the short straw and ended up with the task of disassembling the sticky machines and scrubbing the congealed corn syrup and cheap rum out of every crevice.

Such is the dream job of a shot girl.

Last call doesn't really exist in this city, so the bars close up whenever people stop coming in. Tonight the final group of inebriated bridesmaids wanders back out into the street at half-past three.

"You sure you're alright to finish this on your own, Grace?"

I look up from my spot on the floor, surrounded by metal parts in various stages of gooey to see my co-worker Talia staring at the mess, her brow furrowing as she mentally tries to reassemble the machines.

She unties the turquoise bandana that protects her long braids from backsplash from the drink machines and the hands of grabby tourists. I watch as she combs her fingers through the dark braids, untangling them and smoothing the few baby hairs that had escaped. She twists the simple gold band on her finger unconsciously, and I know that she is already mentally sliding into bed next to her husband to claim a few precious hours of sleep.

We're just starting to blur that line between co-workers and friends, and no one wants to be friends with the needy girl who can't do her own damn work. I shake my head. "Thanks, Talia, but it's fine. They'll be good as new tomorrow. You have to get Sasha up for school in like five hours. Go home."

Rolling her dark eyes, she groans, "Don't remind me. Someone needs to open a school for the kids of bartenders and insomniacs that doesn't start until past noon." She shrugs into a grey hoodie and pauses at the door. "Lock up behind me, and be careful on your way home."

"Yes Mama," I reply, heaving myself up to fasten the deadbolt behind her before returning to the mess on the floor.

By the time the ancient machines are clean and whirring again, it's almost five and the streets are utterly deserted. Pocketing the keys, I yank on the door to make sure the building is secure and try to ignore the prickling on the back of my neck telling me that no matter how empty the streets might look I'm not alone.

Burying my hands in my pockets, I start walking. Parking is a nightmare around here, so I end most nights with a half mile trek to my car. Usually, the walk is a welcome time to wind down after a long shift.

But usually, I'm not acutely aware of the faint footsteps trailing a few blocks behind me.

Probably just another bartender that got stuck late. Or a REALLY late night partier.

Or you're about to get murdered, my traitorous brain helpfully adds.

I quicken my pace, fighting the urge to look over my shoulder.

The steps speed up as well.

My hand closes around the pocket stun gun I bought my first day back in the city, the smooth plastic only slightly reassuring as the footsteps grow louder.

I can see my car in the distance, parked under a burnt out streetlight fifty yards away. Clenching my keys in my other hand, I run.

The clattering of my feet on the uneven pavement and the sound of my own heartbeat blocks out the noise of my pursuer, but I know he's still back there. Frantically pressing the unlock button, I see the headlights blink, and I yank the door open, turning my head as the footsteps abruptly stop.

Nothing.

I'm alone on the street.

I shake my head at myself. Relying on caffeine and adrenaline rather than sleep has me perpetually on edge. I scan the shuttered bars and darkened storefronts once more before climbing inside my car and locking the door, the sharp scent of ozone filling my nose.

Just in case.

MORNING COMES FAR TOO EARLY.

Even as a child, I've always been a light sleeper. Creaks from the old walls settling or wind that hopefully wouldn't roll into another hurricane smacking against the shutters never fails to jerk me into awareness. Once my eyes open, that's it. No more sleep for today.

New Orleans is a lot of things, but quiet definitely isn't one of them. I'd tossed and turned for the better part of an hour, hyper-aware of every noise and half convinced that my mysterious pursuer was creeping up my porch steps.

I finally drifted into a fitful doze close to dawn, filled with restless dreams of broken glass and black wings.

The loud sound of an irritated driver laying on a car horn peels my eyes open far too soon. Rolling over, I squint at the old silver alarm clock ticking merrily on my bedside table.

10:14 AM. Lovely. Four hours of sleep is going to make my shift tonight an absolute *delight*.

Groaning, I crawl out of the tangled mess of red sheets on my bed and pad to the bathroom, the creaks of the hundred-year-old floorboards comforting in their familiarity after last night. Turning the taps onto cold, the pipes moan loudly as the bracingly cold water pours into the white porcelain sink. Splashing the icy water on my face chases away the last dregs of sleep but does little to erase the bone-deep exhaustion that has settled into me in the last few days.

Last night might have been the first time I got scared enough to acknowledge it, but it wasn't the first time I've been followed. Getting stared at is nothing new at my job, but the gazes from frat boys that never look up from my chest don't feel like fingers digging into the back of my skull, demanding I turn around.

I've been ignoring those feelings for a week. Part of me didn't want to risk meeting the eyes of whoever could make my throat tighten with fear from just a look, but a much larger part knew that letting my stalker think I was cheerfully oblivious to his attention was a much safer bet.

Easy enough to do in a crowd, but that cover is most definitely blown now.

A soft meow comes from the kitchen, and I half-sprint the short distance to the room, knowing what I'm going to see. I stand in the doorway, trying to will what's in front of my face to disappear.

The window over my sink gapes open.

I dropped my keys twice last night, my hands shaking too much to fit the key into the lock properly, and when I finally made it inside, I tore through the house, checking and rechecking every window and door to make absolutely sure the house was secure.

I locked the kitchen window first and secured the inner shutter with the latch I rarely bothered to use. The humidity swelled the wood so much over the years that it's a nightmare to open. Opening that shutter is difficult and above all loud. And there's no way to do it from the outside.

Someone was in here while I slept.

The meow sounds again, and I absently bend down and pick up the orange tomcat that made his way into my kitchen. Gabriel is technically a stray, but I started buying him cans of tuna with my spare change the first day I caught him sunning his furry ginger body on my stoop. He follows my every step whenever I'm at home, so I've accepted my new role of cat owner at this point.

I sink down onto one of the kitchen chairs, my brain idly reminding me for the thousandth time that the red wooden chairs could use some cushions. My hand mechanically strokes Gabriel's velvet soft ears, but for once the low rumbles of his purrs does little to relax me.

Sunlight and warmth pours into my kitchen from that open window, but I've never felt colder.

Someone was in here.

I have nowhere else to go. No one I can turn to.

And someone was in here.

THERE'S magic in this city, Gracie-girl, and there's magic in women. A woman in New Orleans? There's nothing we can't do if we set our minds to it. . .

My mother's words echo in my head as I stand in the street, staring at the bright yellow door and the peeling black sign above it that simply reads VOODOO in thick block letters. Carved deep into the yellow wood is a stylized heart with crosses and swirls radiating from the center.

Growing up here, the rituals seep into you as unquestionably as the humidity peels the paint and warps the wood. I never gave the dishes of salt and herbs left on the doorstep or the chalk marks drawn under tables a second thought back then, and this is far from the first time I've ever set foot in a shop like this.

I can see her, all messy golden hair and wide smiles, plucking the fresh herbs from the wild garden she dug in our small backyard and hanging them in doorways to dry into brittle green bunches. She'd pull down the bundles and trek into a shop like this and wait silently until the last tourist filtered out of the dim room before ducking into the back room with her basket of herbs, leaving me mesmerized by the bright trinkets and jewelry lining the counters to lure in the tourists.

Low voices and feminine laughter would filter from behind the curtains, and she would emerge a few minutes later, thick candles or red flannel pouches tucked in her hands. My mother always looked content and prepared when she left those rooms.

Never afraid.

Maybe that's why I'm finding myself in front of this store instead of at the police station. Some part of me knows that whoever is trailing me won't be concerned with a badge or a gun.

I push open the door and step inside the shadowy building.

Like every other occult shop in the city, the air hangs heavy with the thick scent of incense and herbs mixed with just a hint of smoke. Every spare inch of the shelves and counters are crammed with bottles and jars of various mixtures and hand-poured candles, as well as the cheaper mass-produced variety papered with brightly colored images of saints.

"I know what you're here for."

Startled, I turn quickly and see the woman standing behind me, the deep blue beaded curtain separating the main store from the back room flowing around her like water.

She takes another step into the room, her eyes raking my form and I get the distinct feeling she recognizes me. Striking is the only word I can think of to adequately describe her. Taller than me by at least half a foot, her smooth dark skin seems almost luminous in the faint light of the store. Her black hair twists into a braid that wraps around her head, and a deep gold dress formed out of a cascade of ruffles swirls around her feet as she walks.

She barely looks older than I do, but something in her eyes tells a different story.

"You don't quite believe it yet," she says, her low voice drawing out each word as she takes my hand and leads me through that blue curtain, the beads cool as they slip over my shoulders. "You will soon enough, Grace."

"How do you know my name?" I stammer, breaking the trance.

She chuckles, the soft sound almost musical. "Of everything that's happened to you in the last few days, that's what gives you pause?"

"I don't know what to believe anymore."

"Sit." She motions to the simple folding chair set up next to a small round table draped in shades of red and gold and lit by two fat white candles. I sit on the edge of the chair, feeling like that same wide-eyed child following her mother into these shops and wondering what went on behind the curtains.

"I can't tell you everything I'd like to, child. There are rules with this sort of thing, you see," she flutters one of her hands dismissively, the gold rings on her slender fingers glinting in the candlelight. "Not my rules, by any stretch, but we all have our parts to play. You've been through so much already. . ."

She grasps my hand, flipping it over to rest palm up on the table, and she stares at my palm with laser focus.

Almost as an afterthought, she adds, "I knew your mother."

I try to tug my hand away at her words, but her grip holds me like iron. When she looks up at my face, her dark eyes are sad.

"You're afraid. You should be. I know what hunts you."

No part of me is surprised that she said *what* instead of *who*.

One long, bare nail traces a line down the center of my palm. I shiver. "The world has many more layers than you imagine. Good isn't always good. And the blackest evil can be the only light that can cut through the shadows." The low cadence of her voice and the sweet, heady scent of the candlewax makes her words feel like a dream and I can feel my eyes growing heavy. I blink the haze from them, forcing myself back to awareness.

"Why the riddles?" I can't hide the flare of anger that

sparks in me. A few days ago, the only thing I had to worry about was an overdue electric bill, and now I'm apparently being hunted by some supernatural creature. I came here for answers, but instead, I'm just getting more and more questions.

"The world was built on riddles and stories, Grace," she says, her tone growing far less languid and more clipped. "You'll meet him soon enough. Every cell in your body will scream at you to run. Don't. He's the only thing that can protect you now that you're the Last."

"The Last?" I echo, furrowing my brow as I try to make sense of her words. "Who am I supposed to meet?"

She shakes her head, her expression as immovable as the braids wreathing her skull. Rising from the chair, she pulls a small red bag from the folds of her skirt and presses it into my hands. I grip the soft flannel.

"I don't need to tell you what to do with a mojo bag, do I?" Her eyes glimmer with just a bit of amusement as she pulls me to my feet. "Keep it close, and it will buy you a bit of time. It can't protect you forever, but that's where he comes in. You both might just save each other."

She squeezes my hand before ushering me through the front door and back to the street. I find my tongue just before the door closes and ask, "What's your name?"

She hesitates for a moment, and I almost expect her not to tell me.

"Erzulie," she replies before shutting the door and flipping the sign in the window to read CLOSED.

5

LUCIFER

Hell wants me back.

I open my eyes to stare at the sky blue ceiling of the suite I'd procured at The Saint hotel. The irony of the Devil bedding down in the Archangel Michael Suite was too much for my sense of whimsy to resist.

Two curvaceous brunettes sprawl across the bed, tanned limbs and dark hair entangled across the pure white sheets.

Well, not quite so pure anymore.

I rise from the bed and stalk to the window, the plush blue carpet soft beneath my feet as I tug open the curtains and flood the room with bright midday sun.

The city spreads out before me like a feast, but the never-ceasing buzz of human sins in my brain is drowned out by the snarls of demons howling for my return.

Three sharp knocks on the door interrupt my musings.

Odd. I don't remember ordering an interruption.

I yank open the door, ready to unleash my full wrath upon the interloper. Instead, I find myself positively grinning at the familiar face standing on my threshold.

"Hello, Phenex. Fancy meeting you here."

I step aside, letting the slender blond enter the suite.

We do love our titles in Hell, and Phenex is a Marquis with twenty legions of demons under his command. In the early days, he tore his way through the celestial battles, matching blow for blow with the cruelest of the Fallen, but his heart was never truly in it.

I don't need to touch him to learn his deepest desire. Phenex wears it like a shroud everywhere he goes.

He wants to go back.

"This hotel's a bit on the nose, isn't it?" he drawls, settling himself on one of the long white couches. His eyes flick to the bed where one of the girls watches us with sleep-bleary eyes. "They come with the room?"

Rolling my eyes, I turn to the girls. "Out," I order.

They scramble to obey, hastily pulling on last night's dresses and too-high heels, albeit more than a little reluctantly. "We can come back later," the taller of the two adds, her gaze moving from Phenex to myself.

I chuckle at her mental salivations. "Now now Clare, your husband probably wouldn't appreciate it if you spent yet another night out getting Eiffel towered instead of cooking him dinner. Adultery is such a petty little sin. Maybe invite Jamie here over one night instead. Men never seem too bothered by that brand of adultery," I add with a smirk.

Her mouth hangs open for a moment with misplaced moral indignation before she grabs her friend's arm and bolts from the suite, slamming the door on her exit.

"She seemed nice."

Phenex makes himself comfortable, propping his feet up on the glass coffee table, the cream-colored alligator hide of his boots fitting in surprisingly well with the absurd opulence of the room. Sprawled across the white fabric, Phenex makes a striking figure. He always looked a bit too angelic for Hell, and that was never more apparent than now.

A fallen angel in a white seersucker suit? Even for New Orleans that might be a bit much.

"Why are you here?"

The bored prettyboy affectation drops immediately. "Why are you here?" he counters, rising to his feet in one smooth motion.

Phenex stands toe to toe with me. Smaller than me in height and muscle mass, Phenex has little chance of besting me even in a mortal fistfight. On the field of battle, I could obliterate him in an instant.

"The souls." I always liked Phenex. Once the first angelic battles ended, he left the violence to the Fallen that reveled in it, pouring himself into the subtler sins of vanity and lust while the wrathful around him filled Hell with torrents of blood in a misguided effort to curry my favor.

The solemn look on Phenex's face splits into a broad smile, and he slaps my arm. "And I'm here to help you, brother." Ever curious, Phenex leaves my side and prowls around the room, inspecting the random artifacts scattered across the suite for decoration before pausing at the window and staring unseeingly across the city.

"You're not the only one who needed a bit of shore leave, Lucifer." He sighs, and I hear a millennia of regret in that exhalation. "Hope is a deception for someone like me. I'm not a fool, despite what the others think. I know Heaven won't have me back."

I always told myself that reigning in Hell is worth the loss of Heaven to me. The one commonality I had with Michael and his ilk was the refusal to be a servant to those that were lesser. But there are so many like Phenex who long for nothing more complex than authority and approval and a place to fit in the divine scheme of existence.

And for the first time, I feel the smallest pang of regret for drawing him into my web all those years ago.

What's past is past though, and I have Hell's future to consider.

"All right," I agree, and Phenex's pensive expression melts into the familiar impish grin. No doubt Phenex's mind is already thinking about which local flavors he wants to sample.

"Business before amusement," I say, snapping him back to the present. "Michael's behind this. No one else has the power. He'll sense we're here soon enough. When he does, don't even try to get in the way, Phenex." My fingers ache to hold my sword at the thought of finally facing down my smarmy ass of a brother after all these centuries.

This time I won't be the one slinking back to be locked away.

This time Michael is *mine*.

"Let's go."

6

GRACE

Something is off.

To most, today would seem like just another day. Jazz music filters out of the bars that are already doing a brisk business despite it barely being noon. The street hawkers aggressively peddle their wares to clueless out-of-towners. The sweet scent of frying beignets wafts through the air, carried on thick humidity.

Even a day ago, I would have ignored the cold knot of dread in my stomach that screamed *wrong*, but those few minutes inside Erzulie's shop ripped the veil from my eyes.

I can see, but even more importantly, I can *feel*.

A young couple tries to push past a man selling t-shirts on the sidewalk. From one second to the next, his jovial grin curls into a snarl and he grabs the man's arm, shoving him back into the display and collapsing the flimsy card table, piles of cheap purple cotton falling on the ground around him.

I stop, almost trembling at the pure rage I feel coming from the man. The ever-present police that wander Bourbon Street are absent, and I watch helplessly as he curls his fingers around the smaller man's neck and drags him up, oblivious to the shrieks of his victim's girlfriend. He glances over his shoulder and sees me.

His eyes are pure black.

Like an afterthought, he drops his intended victim like a rag doll and stalks toward me. His head cocks to the side like a curious animal.

I take a step back, the confidence from the little red mojo bag stuffed in my purse draining away as I stare into those dead black eyes. Every instinct tells me to run, but my feet stay riveted to the spot as that *thing* dressed up as a man inches closer.

"Now now, it's a bit early for senseless violence, isn't it?"

The creature immediately stops its advance at the bored-sounding voice, the black eyes focusing on the figure behind me. I turn to see two men watching the scene play out.

They are a study in contrast standing next to each other. The smaller of the two men leans against a lamppost, watching the whole terrifying scenario with bright blue eyes that seem to glint in amusement at it all. He looks like one of the golden boys of Tulane, much more likely to spend his days lazing in one of the French Quarter mansions rather than dirtying himself on Bourbon in his immaculate white suit.

Cherubic, my mind absently supplies the word, but despite his flawless good looks, my eyes are drawn to his companion.

Oh.

He wears a black suit that hugs his muscular frame like a second skin, and he moves with the gait of a predator as he steps around me. Just a hint of stubble darkens the tanned skin of his chiseled jaw, and my eyes unwillingly follow the contours of his face, tracing razor-sharp cheekbones up to eyes dark enough to swallow the light.

He touches my arm as he crosses in front of me, blocking the assailant that I genuinely forgot about. "Maybe later, sweetheart," he says idly. When his fingers brush my arm, he falters in his step, his attention snapping from the black-eyed man to me in an instant.

"How?" he asks, his fingers tightening around my wrist as he stares into my eyes as if searching for something.

"Planning on taking care of that anytime soon, brother?" Annoyance flashes across his features as the blond's comment pulls us both back to reality. He lingers just a moment longer, his fingers warm against my pulse before letting me go and turning back to our little problem.

"You're one of mine," he growls, stalking toward the creature who stands perfectly still, its black eyes watching him almost expectantly. "A nasty one too. All that rage just boiling over with no real form anymore. And you're just the start," he mutters to himself. "You know where you belong. I have better things to do than collect each one of you," he spits, closing the last foot between them and pressing his palm against its forehead.

The blackness drains out of its eyes, leaving a perfectly normal shade of brown in its wake, and the man slumps to the ground looking dazed.

"You're one of mine."

His words repeat in my head. He's the one who turned a perfectly normal person into a monster in the space of an eye blink.

I take a step backward, willing his focus to stay off me for just another moment as I slip through the crowd that grew around us. Thankful for the love of any spectacle that constantly permeates New Orleans, I push my way through the gawkers and duck into an alleyway.

I follow the winding back streets, walking as fast as I dare.

Don't run. If you run, that gives them a reason to chase you.

I put half a dozen blocks between myself and the scene

before I allow myself to stop. I lean against the wall, the cool dampness of the stone soaking through my dress as I try and fail to make myself stop shaking.

Power.

It poured off him in waves. He stopped that creature like it was nothing, ripping out whatever had infected that man with the ease of pulling out a splinter.

"And you're just the start."

7

LUCIFER

"Where did she go?"

The crowd disperses slowly around us, the curious onlookers searching for their amusement elsewhere as soon as it became apparent that the scene had ended.

Phenex arches an eyebrow at my question. "That little blonde? She ran off." He nudges the unconscious lump of a man crumpled on the ground with the toe of his boot. "So this is what we have to look forward to then?"

I nod. Physically he'll be fine, but mentally is another story. Possession always leaves scars on the host, but at least demons know how to worm their way into a victim slowly.

These trapped souls have all the finesse of a jackhammer. Those scant few minutes trapped inside his own head with that soul will leave him with a case of PTSD that will haunt him for the rest of his days. And there will be others.

I scan the crowd, searching every face for the tell-tale blackness that covers the infected like a haze and see nothing. It's just beginning, but even I can't be everywhere at once.

I spare one last glance at the man on the ground.

Greed. Short-changing a few tourists.

Lust. Telling the wife he was working late while sneaking off for a lap dance.

Envy. Laughing when his neighbor's shiny little convertible was stolen.

Before today, his sins were small time, barely a blip on the celestial radar. His halo might not have been the brightest, but he certainly wasn't one of mine yet, but I can already see the changes in him.

Humans have tried to describe the soul for as long as they've had language, but *Pulp Fiction* came the closest in recent years to getting it right. Every angel, Fallen or otherwise, can see into a mortal's soul with just a touch, but none with the clarity that I can. Sins, memories, their most naked desires – they're all laid bare before me.

I am the Lightbringer, and those souls are brighter than the sun until evil creeps into them and slowly blackens that purity. Veins of blackness are already twisting through that unfortunate mortal's soul, far darker than his petty sins would have caused. It will only spread more as time passes, infecting him with the violence and cruelty of that broken spirit that wore him like a cheap suit.

Michael just damned another human to my realm.

"I hope it was worth it," I mutter bitterly before turning back to Phenex.

"It's going to get worse. Exponentially worse."

Phenex stands stiffly next to me; his perpetual humor finally silenced as the soldier in him waits for orders.

"Find Michael."

Silence.

Nothingness.

Just pure white light.

I thought nothing of the diminutive blonde frozen in terror at the sight of my lovely possessed friend until my fingers closed around her arm. I expected to hear the same sins I hear from every privileged American college girl – binge drinking, cheating on exams, maybe an illicit affair with a married professor.

I expected her to be nothing more than a pretty diversion to while away my downtime as I searched for Michael.

I didn't expect this.

This is something new.

I have to find her.

With Phenex scouring the city for any sign of Michael, I can afford to indulge my curiosity. If I run across a few more errant souls in my search, even better.

This part of New Orleans is a maze of narrow side streets and wider thoroughfares, all choked with humans eager to glut themselves on everything the city offers. I weave my way through the crowd, a shark among minnows, my mind idly ticking off petty crimes.

Sloth. A young man with bloodshot eyes, lazing away his 20s in a cloud of marijuana smoke.

Wrath. A clean-cut preacher with a broad smile who beats his wife every night.

Pride. A trophy wife sneering at a panhandler.

Cataloging humanity's failings is as unconscious for me as breathing, but unless I run across something particularly nasty they barely register on their own.

The preacher will end up as one of mine someday. Cruelty and hypocrisy always come to the same end.

I can feel her. She's close.

I follow my instincts, oblivious to humans jostling each other around me, their forgotten sins not even registering in my thoughts anymore as the beacon draws me closer.

I end up outside yet another bar, one of those terminally hip locations where this decade's version of yuppies go to preen and pound back $16 cocktails.

She sits perched on a stool at the end of the bar, her head in her hands and a mass of golden curls obscuring her face. Her purse is flung carelessly on the stool next to her, an obvious ploy to prevent the middle management Lotharios prowling the room from sitting next to her. The simple leather tote hangs open, and I see a small red flannel bag poking out the top.

Of course. Voodoo. When in New Orleans, after all.

I sit down on the next stool, and a shiver goes through her small frame as I draw closer.

Perceptive, this one.

Slowly she lifts her head, resignation written across her pretty face.

"You found me," she says dully.

"You wanted me to." I reach into her bag and snatch the little flannel pouch out, tearing the hastily stitched closure open.

"Don't!" she protests, "I need that!" I pause, curiosity getting the better of me. She obviously has no idea what's inside this bag. "It's supposed to protect me. From you."

I chuckle as I pour out the bag's contents.

Just as I thought.

Instead of the usual jumble of herbs and stones, only a heavy iron coin falls into my palm. I turn it over, my thumb tracing the sharp angles of the sigil carved into both sides.

"What is that?" she asks. Barely a quaver in her voice this time. The proximity of so many others lessens her fear bit by bit, and she reaches across the empty seat and plucks the coin from my hand. She narrows her eyes as she examines the symbol. "What does this symbol mean?"

"It's my sigil." If this girl is a witch or a medium, she's certainly not very good at it.

"And who are you?"

"Lucifer," I reply, smirking inwardly as her eyes widen at my utterance of the word that froze the blood of untold amounts of mortals.

"Wow," she murmurs. Despite the oddness of our initial meeting, I prepare myself for the usual onslaught of fear tempered with just the perfect amount of lust.

Instead, laughter bubbles out of those lacquered pink lips, and her deep grey eyes hold a note of desperate amusement.

She doesn't believe me.

"Your parents never even gave you a chance did they?"

"You're right about that," I reply dryly, signaling the bartender for a drink. An instant later a heavy tumbler of top-shelf whiskey appears in front of me.

Bit by bit, the smile fades from her face as her mind no doubt ticks off every observation in the brief minutes she's spent in my presence.

"You're serious?"

"As a heart attack." I turn in my seat, leaning back against the edge of the bar and survey the room as I sip my whiskey. Fight or flight wars with each other inside this inquisitive girl. She isn't making a move to run just yet so I soldier on.

"You seem to have me at a disadvantage. You know who I am, but I find myself at a loss to figuring out who you are. And I don't much care for not knowing."

"I'm Grace."

"Of course you are." Dropping my glass on the bar with a heavy clunk, I grab her arm without looking at her, catching her with the speed of a striking snake.

Nothing.

I press deeper into her mind, searching for the walls that the more powerful out there might put up to block my presence. Those walls always have cracks that I can tear through with enough pressure, but there is nothing. No walls. No hidden doors. Just pure white light that I haven't seen since-

Heaven.

"What are you?" I hiss.

She jerks her arm out of my grip, and I let her. "I'm not anyone," she snaps.

"I very much doubt that. You couldn't keep me out if you were no one." At her searching look, I scan the room settling on a tall man in an off the rack suit flirting heavily with a busty blonde in a yellow dress painted onto her generous curves. Without contact, I won't get quite the same Technicolor detail of their lives, but it's close enough to paint my new friend an acceptable picture of my abilities.

"See those two over in the corner table?" Grace casually looks over her shoulder, her nose wrinkling at the sight of the man. "You know him?"

She shakes her head. "I know the type. Entitled. Thinks he can buy whatever he wants, including her."

"Well, he's correct there. She's an escort. She'd do well to avoid him though. He's cheap. He'll find a way to weasel out of paying her, even if he has to rob her after the transaction is completed." The girl tosses her head back, fake laughter ringing across the bar as she squeezes her companion's arm. "Theft isn't very high on the list of sins, but you're right about the entitlement. The world owes him as far as he's concerned, and soon enough he might get the balls to take what he thinks he deserves. It won't end pretty for whichever girl he sets his sights on then. He'll be one of mine."

Grace falls silent next to me, her fingers tearing the bar napkin into damp confetti. "So you can read people's souls just by looking at them?"

"Physical contact gets me more detail, but I can see the gist from here."

I can see the implications of my words swirling in her head. Abruptly she asks, "Why are you telling me this?"

Something about this young and very human-seeming girl make me want to eschew the usual deceptions. I actually find myself wanting to be *honest* with her.

"Because you're something new. When I touched your arm earlier, I saw nothing. No past, no future. Just white." I reach up and push an errant curl behind her ear, letting my fingertips brush her cheek just to reassure myself for the third time of the truth.

"So does that mean I don't have a soul?" she blurts out, her brow creasing as she ponders the implications of lacking something she likely didn't believe in a few hours ago.

"I very much doubt that as well. You have divine blood somewhere in your line, powerful enough that thousands of years of dilution with mortals hasn't erased it."

I pause, studying her face with an intensity that clearly makes her uncomfortable. The flush in her cheeks has very little to do with the heat outside or her frantic attempt to escape me. I follow that heated skin to the hollow of her collarbone and lower, to where it disappears under the brighter red of her sundress.

I smirk as I ponder just how far down I'm making her blush.

"I wonder," I murmur, thinking out loud as Grace squirms under my scrutiny. "I'd almost think you were an offshoot of one of my brothers, but you don't have the touch of madness about you. Nephilim never last for much time in the world. A bit too crazy to keep a low enough profile to survive."

She stays surprisingly calm through my narrative, and for the first time, I find myself wanting to know what is swirling inside a human's brain.

"Definitely not Nephilim. Even if you managed to be the first in history that wasn't utterly batshit, you still would have been hunted down already, especially with Archangels skulking around the city."

Her entire body goes still at the word *hunted*. So then, I'm not the only person intrigued by this little blonde.

"Someone is hunting me. Or something." Her slender fingers still toy with the iron coin, nervously tracing and retracing the sigil carved into it.

I wonder if any part of her notices the shiver of power that comes from her fingertips each time she draws my symbol.

She continues on, oblivious to the slowly warming coin in her hand. "When I saw you in the square, I thought it was you. But I think you're someone else."

She tries futilely to signal the bartender, the rocks glass at her elbow holding nothing more than watery dregs, her voice lost in the crowd of alcohol-seekers.

Sighing, I push my nearly full glass toward her. This one needs some liquid courage.

She smiles gratefully and takes a delicate sip of the smoky bourbon, her eyes fluttering shut for just a moment as the savors the drink.

"I think we were supposed to meet. Someone made sure that I would find you. . . or that you would find me. She told me, '*The blackest evil can be the only light that can cut through the shadows.*'" Grace laughs, a bitterness in her tone that sounds wrong on someone so young.

What damage has Heaven already done to her?

"Somehow I didn't expect the Devil to be the one who's supposed to protect me. She certainly left that part out."

My suspicions grow as she describes the riddles she's been fed about our foretold meeting.

"I think we might have a mutual acquaintance," I say, stealing my drink back from her hand for a long sip as I recall those ageless eyes and the words she hissed at me in the middle of the street.

I fucking hate prophecies.

"'He's coming for her. And you aren't strong enough to stop him. He'll tear you apart, one feather at a time if you get in his way. And you'll get in his way,'" I parrot. "I thought the old woman was just another charlatan fortune teller at first, but she knew who I was. And I think she knows you as well."

The color drains from her skin at my words, replacing that enticing blush with an unhealthy pallor. I press the drink back into her palm, my fingers steadying her trembling hand as she grips the glass.

"She wasn't old," Grace replies, fighting to keep her voice even. "She barely looked 30, but she said she knew my mother."

Unsurprising. Someone playing with these kinds of forces isn't just another witch. "Did she tell you her name? I never got the pleasure."

Grace hesitates, and that momentary distrust makes me respect her just a bit more. Divine blood or not, she is a young, breakable mortal. Her very life is being toyed with by forces that vastly overpower her, but she still isn't about to hitch herself to the first potential protector that might come along.

"She said her name was Erzulie."

I snort. "I don't know what else I expected in New Orleans. She's a loa. The spirit of beauty, luxury and love and the protector of women and children, if I recall."

I notice that my hand is still covering Grace's, even though hers has long since stopped shaking. I jerk my hand back abruptly. "I'm not surprised she's irritated at the Archangels stomping around her territory," I add.

"I still don't know what this all has to do with me." The fear drains out of her, replaced with a weariness that I recognize all too well. She picks up the coin from the bar again, turning it over in her hand as though the sharp angles of my symbol hold the answers she needs. "I'm no one. I'm just a girl working at a shitty bar with dead parents and too much student loan debt. And now I can't even go home because whoever is following me was *in my house*." She looks up from the coin, her eyes shining when they meet mine, but she blinks the tears away before they can fall. "But along with all that, apparently I'm the Last, whatever that means."

Time freezes around us.

Not really, of course. The bartender still pours drinks, twisting fruit into elaborate garnishes and handing them off to the doe-eyed waitress who fantasizes about leaving her husband for him. Directly to my right a couple is on a first date, all giggles and furtive glances at each other. Across the bar, the lovely escort in the yellow dress is inches from throwing a drink in Mr. Entitlement's face.

But all of it fades into silence around me as I realize just why the Archangels want this girl and just what they will go through to obliterate her.

8

GRACE

The Devil is in my house.

The fucking *Devil* is in my *house*.

For all the bizarre, terrifying turns my life has taken in the last twenty-four hours, it's safe to say that the absolute last way I expected to end my day was with Lucifer sitting at my kitchen table, watching me with a look that can only be described as apprehension.

The instant the words "I'm the Last" leave my mouth, Lucifer's entire demeanor changes. Gone is the casually inquisitive and slightly lecherous gaze. He goes still next to me, tension coiling in his muscles as his eyes dart around the room.

"We should get out of here." False levity colors his low voice, and his lips pull in a tight smile that's dangerously close to a grimace. If my words managed to make the Devil this nervous, I'm guessing that I'm pretty well screwed.

Once we exit the cool interior of the bar, Lucifer wastes no time in flagging down a cab, scrutinizing the driver for an instant before tugging me into the battered yellow car.

"Don't you have wings?" I ask, only half joking.

One side of Lucifer's mouth quirks into a smile that doesn't quite reach his eyes. "I never bring out the wings on a first date. You have to leave some mystery."

I rattle off my address to the driver and lean back onto the worn leather seat, trying to reconcile the fact that this seemingly normal, if devastatingly sexy, man next to me is the actual Devil.

The cabbie drives with the same level of reckless abandon everyone in this city adopts after a few months. Lucifer stares out the window through the drive, seeming to scan the face of everyone we pass while darting quick glances back at me as though he expects something to reach through the cab window and snatch me.

We pull to the curb in front of my house. Before I touch the door handle, Lucifer is out and opening it for me and ushering me up the steps. He calls over his shoulder at the cabbie, "Consider this as penance for overcharging that poor couple from Nebraska last night!"

Gabriel is sunning himself at the top of the steps. Lucifer pauses, cocking his head as the cat fixes him with a bored gaze before standing up and twining himself through my legs.

"I'm glad you don't have a dog," Lucifer says, bending down to scratch the top of Gabriel's head. "Dogs don't care for my kind much. Cats though? Their no fucks philosophy meshes quite well with my own."

My hands are steady as I unlock my front door. Lucifer stands at my back, so close that I can feel his body heat and smell the scent of his skin, smoke and some unnamed spice.

I ease open my door, and Gabriel runs inside, his paws nearly silent on the wood floors. Lucifer follows at my heels, pushing the door closed behind us and clicking the lock and deadbolt. I open my mouth to make a joke about how we could rig up a barricade if he really wants to but the words die in my throat at the look on his face.

Whatever is after me, it's bad.

Desperate for even the barest semblance of normalcy, I walk into the kitchen where Gabriel sits expectantly by his empty bowl, gazing at me with the level of disdain only a hungry cat can muster. Lucifer sits down on one of my kitchen chairs, watching without comment as I rummage through my cabinets in search of a can of cat food.

I've just opened the can, wrinkling my nose at the pungent smell, when Lucifer breaks the silence.

"You're the Last. I know exactly what that means."

I unceremoniously dump the food into Gabriel's bowl and sink down into the chair opposite Lucifer, forcing myself to abandon any more ploys to delay his revelation.

"What you are is not just a girl working at a shitty bar with dead parents and too much student loan debt." He repeats my own words back to me, his dark eyes boring into mine with a look of complete certainty. He doesn't need to read my soul to know the truth. "What you are is God's great-great-great-ad infinitum granddaughter."

I always considered myself an articulate person. You don't survive graduate-level journalism classes without a decent grasp of the English language. But all that schooling and every witty comeback I've ever prided myself on melts away and all I can think to say is a deeply eloquent, "What?"

"You know the stories. Virgin birth, son of God, blah blah blah," Lucifer leans back in his chair, a posture that would appear relaxed to a casual observer, but I don't miss the way his eyes track the room, pausing at each window and doorway. "What you don't know, what no one but the angels knows is that Mary's virgin birth was twins. Everyone knows what happened to the boy. But the girl? She wasn't exactly born into a world known for fair treatment of women.

"Mary might have been innocent in some aspects, but she was far from stupid. She knew that whatever role her son might play in history wouldn't favor her daughter so she gave the sort of sacrifice that only a mother could. She sent the girl away and never saw her again. The girl lived a life. Married, had children, and eventually died. To an outsider, she was shockingly normal, but any angel, Fallen or otherwise, could sense what she was.

"She bore two sons, but they don't matter. You couldn't trace lineage accurately through a male until the last few decades. Who they were and what they did is long since lost and forgotten."

"Then how—"

Lucifer continues as though I haven't said a word. "She had a daughter. And you are of that bloodline."

He falls silent, giving me time to absorb his words.

It can't be true.

I'm not some magical person with holy blood.

I'm just Grace.

This has to be some kind of mistake.

"It's not a mistake," Lucifer says, his voice shockingly gentle. He reaches across the kitchen table and presses his hand over my own, stroking the back of my hand as though soothing a skittish animal. "I'm not wrong. You're not having a psychotic break. This isn't a dream or a joke."

His voice grows harder as he returns to his story. He doesn't take his hand away. "Nephilim were always considered an abomination. Mixing divine blood with human? God got a pass for that one time because. . . God," he says with a shrug. "But any angels who stepped out of line and did the same? It didn't end so well for them or their offspring."

"But if the angels could sense her from the beginning why did they let her survive?" I counter, still trying to wrap my head around this insane theological discussion I'm having at my kitchen table with *Lucifer*.

Lucifer shakes his head. "Things were different back then.

My absentee Father was much more present, and the angels were loathe to step out of line. They didn't dare touch her. As time passed the divinity in that bloodline faded to nothingness in her sons, but it stayed in her daughter and her daughter's daughter and so on. But when God fell silent, the Archangels took it upon themselves to interpret the rules."

I feel the cold creeping into my body, and every part of me wants to scream for him to stop talking. To not ask the words I know are coming next.

"How did your parents die?"

I shake my head. "No," I beg, not caring how broken my voice sounds. "It was a car accident. It was just a random terrible thing that happened." I stare at Lucifer's hand on mine, barely seeing it, and try to ignore the hot tears that slip down my cheeks.

"Someone killed them."

"Yes." Flat. Final. Someone murdered my family, and all he can say is *Yes*.

"Grace, look at me." Slowly I lift my head, expecting to see pity but instead Lucifer's features twist into a look of pure rage. His face softens after a moment, the hate draining from his features as quickly as it appeared. "Your father was collateral damage. Just something in the way. He was after your mother and you. He wanted to wipe the last traces of your tainted blood from the world. And now he's back to finish the job."

I pull my hand out from under Lucifer's and swipe at my eyes, wiping away the tears and pushing down that small, sad part of me that just wants to curl into a ball and sob.

When I speak again, I barely recognize my own voice.

"Who killed them?"

The smile that crosses Lucifer's lips has nothing to do with any crumb of happiness. "The same person I'm looking for. The Archangel Michael."

Lucifer leans forward, sitting in the same chair my mother once did and resting his arms on the table my father built with his own hands. I feel the last bit of fear drain from me, replaced by something harder. Little Gracie who jumps at shadows is gone.

"I'm going to kill him," Lucifer says, searching my face for any signs of hesitation and finding none.

"Want to help?"

❧ 9 ❧

LUCIFER

The Last.

I expected many things to happen here. I dreamed of a respite, however brief, from the endless screams that echoed through Hell and the tang of iron that perpetually hung in the air. I pictured the persistent crowds of humanity encroaching on my consciousness with their sins and desires. I even envisioned enjoying it, throwing myself into this base, flesh-filled world.

I never imagined her.

She sits silently, absorbing the life-shattering revelation I have just given her. The tears have long since dried on her cheeks, and even the flare of hard anger I saw light up those grey eyes has gone out.

She looks hollow.

This won't do.

I grasp her hand, and I feel her tense at the contact. Good. She's still in there after all.

"You can't stay here." She blinks, and her eyes finally seem to focus on mine. "You cannot stay here," I repeat, emphasizing each word with a forcefulness that would have even the highest ranking demons in Hell scrambling to obey.

Instead, she pulls her hand back and gives me a withering look that would amuse me if not for our current situation.

I certainly know where that particular trait comes from.

"Where the hell am I supposed to go?" she snaps, "This is my home. Michael's apparently taken everything else from me, and now I have to run?"

"You have to survive." I stand up, the chair scraping loudly on the floor, the noise sharp and grating in the silence of the room. "Divine blood or not, you're human. You cannot even begin to comprehend the power an Archangel wields." I lean forward and let the guise of the smirking, flirtatious Devil slip away. "Would you care for a taste?"

Let her get a glimpse of what is behind the mask, and see how eager she is to stay.

The temperature in the room plummets, and I hear thunder roaring in the distance as though nature is rebelling against my very presence.

Few mortals can look upon an angel's true form and survive, and even fewer escape altogether unscathed. If I'm wrong about her, my true face will be the last she sees as her eyes burn away in their sockets.

I'm not wrong.

But there is still room for surprises.

Pure, blinding light bathes the room as my real form overtakes the human guise I wear. Behind me, the shadows of my wings rise up the walls. I can feel my fingers clawing grooves into the wood of the small table separating us as I free just enough of myself to give her a sense of what she's facing.

Grace stands up slowly, her wide-eyed gaze never leaving my own. Instead of backing away and trembling in fear she takes a step closer to me, her face bathed in light. Her small, human hand rises of its own accord and touches my cheek.

Her hand is steady. "So bright," she murmurs, wonderment coloring her tone. "You were called the Lightbringer, weren't you?"

"I still am." Outside the house, I can hear every car alarm on the street sounding as glass cracks and splinters at the power of my true voice. Only inches away from me, Grace doesn't flinch. "The Devil doesn't come dressed in a red cape and horns. He comes as everything you've ever wished for."

"You're right about that," she says, echoing my words from back at the bar. Her hand trails down my face, her fingertips with their chipped blue polish just brushing the skin of my jaw. "I should be afraid of you. Every sane part of me wants to jump in my car and just keep driving until I can forget about angels and devils and holy blood." I hold my tongue and let her continue. "But some other part of me recognizes you. . . knows you."

Her hand drops to her side. When the contact between us breaks Grace takes a slow breath, almost looking as though she's waking from a dream. "So this is what I'm up against then?"

"No," I say, sliding back behind my mask as easily as slipping on a coat. "That was the smallest fraction of what an angel is capable of. I didn't think you'd appreciate me smashing every window on the block."

She glances at the long crack bisecting the window above her kitchen sink and smiles wryly. "Thanks for that." She pauses, her eyes circling the room as though trying to memorize it.

"Take whatever is important to you. I can't guarantee you'll be able to return here anytime soon."

Grace nods. I watch as she grabs a large metal mixing bowl from one of the cabinets and fills it to the brim with dry cat food. She scoops the cat up and carries him through the door, depositing them both on the front porch.

She kneels down next to the cat, scratching the purring animal's head. Her soft voice filters back to me. "I hope you're still here when I come back– *if* I come back," she whispers. A moment later she strides past me into her bedroom, her face carefully impassive.

I follow, leaning against the doorframe and watching as she frantically shoves as much of her life as she can into a worn leather bag. When the suitcase is filled almost to bursting, she yanks the zipper closed and pauses, steeling herself for the next step.

"I'm ready."

———

PHENEX IS LOUNGING on the couch when I open the door to the suite, looking far too comfortable for our current situation. His gaze slips past me and focuses on Grace as she enters the room, the familiar, lustful grin twisting his lips as he looks her up and down.

"What happened to business before amusement?" he drawls. "Not that I mind, but she hardly looks big enough to share."

Grace tenses, and unexpected anger surges through me. A few hours ago I would have chuckled at Phenex's comment. Instead, I find myself fighting the urge to backhand him.

Something about this girl is making me feel *protective*. It's unnerving to say the least.

Always perceptive, Phenex's smirk drains away at my demeanor. "Who is she?" he asks, all traces of humor gone.

"The Last."

Whatever Phenex might be expecting, it isn't that.

He lets out a low whistle as he get to his feet. "I'd ask if you were joking, but. . . I can see it now." Phenex stares at her with open wonder, seeing a relic of the Heaven he has forsaken instead of a living, breathing person. "She almost glows, doesn't she?" he murmurs to himself. "But it's subdued. Like hiding a candle under a box."

Grace steps around me and extends her hand to Phenex. "I'm Grace. And I'm guessing you're not Michael."

Phenex huffs in indignation. "Certainly not," he replies, taking Grace's offered hand. "Michael is a stuck-up tightass with no appreciation of the finer things you humans have to offer. I'm Phenex."

Releasing Grace's hand, Phenex turns his attention back to me. "It can't be a coincidence - Michael, the souls, her presence. I just can't figure out if the souls are the bait or she is."

"Michael's hunting her. He suspects she's the Last, but he never did like getting his hands dirty unless he was certain. We need to keep her hidden."

"Could I actually get included in this conversation?"

We both turn to Grace. Perched on the arm of the couch, she looks fragile.

Breakable.

Far too human.

But at a closer gaze, anyone with perception will see the power flowing through her, simmering just under the surface until something awakes it.

And she is making me *feel* things.

"Please, give us your insight on how to locate and destroy the Archangel who just happens to be God's chosen warrior." At my harsh words, Grace flinches as though I hit her, and I tamp down the desire to reassure. Coddling her will get her one thing – dead. The silence stretches between us as I dare her to speak.

"I thought so." Effectively dismissing her, I turn back to Phenex. "What did you find?"

"Nothing of importance. Just your usual parade of sinners.

Michael seems to be laying low for the moment." His gaze keeps flickering to Grace, watching us silently as we decide her future. "I can think of one thing that might draw him out."

"No," I snap.

Phenex persists. "If she's what he's after it makes sense."

"The answer is no. She is something far too valuable to risk as bait." Out of the corner of my eye, I see Grace bristling at our failure to consult her, but she stays silent. Good. Let her be angry at the situation, at Michael, at *me*. She'll need to tap into a well of pure fury if she has any hopes of survival.

"I need to make myself visible," I say. "Michael never could resist a challenge, especially not from me. If we go to ground, he'll think we're afraid. He'll be too busy congratulating himself to notice that the world's burning around him. But if we act like nothing's amiss and we're just here sampling the local flavor? He'll be incensed that we aren't cowering." Disdain drips from my every word.

Phenex keeps stealing glances at Grace. He opens his mouth, argument on the tip of his tongue before closing it and nodding with reluctant acceptance.

Grace hasn't moved. She stares at me, those grey eyes holding my gaze with an intensity that no mortal could muster.

Just what will it take to cut the last threads of humanity that tie her down? So much power flows just below the surface. She'll rival an Archangel when it awakes.

She'll be a fine weapon.

Until then though, I need to keep her safe.

"Stay put," I order, not giving her an opening to argue.

GRACE

I leave.

I don't know what I expected from Lucifer. I'm not naïve enough to think myself his match in this fight, but I want to do something more than sit quietly in a hotel room while he hunts my family's murderer.

All because I'm something far too valuable to be risked as bait.

To the angels, I'm a thing. Something to be protected or used but not an equal. Never an equal.

They leave me behind to search the city, Lucifer ordering me to "stay put" like I'm a pet.

Sit.

Stay.

Play dead.

Lucifer has his own vendetta against Michael and the rest of Heaven, and he no doubt thinks he's shielding me from the wrath of angels, but there's no way I'm sitting on the sidelines of my own life anymore.

As an afterthought, I dig the little red flannel bag from

the recesses of my purse and tuck the iron coin in my pocket before rushing after them.

TRACKING two men on foot in a city this size is easier said than done. By the time I reach the street, they're both long gone. I pause in the doorway of The Saint, scanning the packed streets for any signs of the two fallen angels and coming up empty.

I glance over my shoulder at the glass doorway that would take me back to the hotel, to the comfortable room where I could wait in relative safety for my future to unfold around me.

No. Not this time. Not ever again.

Instead, I duck out into the crowd, my feet finding the well-trod path that I've followed far too many times in the last few weeks, seeking the cold comfort that only the dead can bring.

The iron gates of Lafayette Cemetery loom ahead, and I follow the path, the stones under my feet cracked from the endless parade of tourists that come to gawk at the city of the dead.

The cemetery is quiet today. I pass the familiar tombs, idly ticking off Augustin, Bellard, and Cavaille before I reach Celestin.

The family mausoleum is large, one of the few that is a small building rather than just an above-ground grave. Tucked in one of the lesser used thoroughfares of the cemetery, it escapes the notice of most passersby.

A stone angel perches on the peaked roof, staring coldly down at me as I slip into the chilly darkness.

Funny, I used to find that angel's presence comforting.

Out of habit, I run my fingers over the verse carved into the arching doorway.

> Fear not
> I am the first and the Last
> I am she that liveth, and was dead
> and, behold, I am alive for evermore
> and have the keys of Hell and of death.

Revelations. As a teenager, I'd ascribed the gender change in the verse on an ancestor more concerned with female pride than possible blasphemy, but beyond that bit of trivia, I paid no attention to the words. I press my fingertips against *Last*, the cool dampness of the stone sinking into my skin.

She knew. They all knew.

I sink down on the stone bench that rests in the center of the mausoleum, trying to wrap my head around the realization that my mother knew the truth of our bloodline and made the choice to hide it from me.

Name after name lines the tombs.

Arelia

Genevieve

Rose

Serafine

All Celestin. Not a single woman in our family has ever taken her husband's name.

The few men buried here all bore different last names.

Ducrest

Lacour

Anderson

And then there are the two tombs closest to the back - the stone newer, the sheen of the modern hewn marble still only a few years old.

Marianne Celestin

William Murphy

"Hi, Mom. Hi, Dad," I say, softly. "So things have gotten pretty crazy in the past few days. I met someone who seems to know more about my family than I do." I fall silent, staring unseeingly at the quiet stone, breathing in the faint smell of decay from last week's wilting roses.

"I don't know why I thought I would get answers here. I guess I just felt like this would be a safe place to think." Almost unconsciously I pull Lucifer's coin from my pocket, my fingertips making the now familiar circuit of the angular symbol.

"How is Lucifer the only person who has been honest with me in my entire life?" I demand. "How could you keep this from me?"

Hindsight always is 20/20, and when I think back to my carefree teenage years, there are so many little isolated events that all lead back to this tomb and the cursed Celestin bloodline.

Talismans of faiths that most of the world has long forgotten always filled our house. Once a pencil rolled across the floor, and a quick glance upward while retrieving it revealed an elaborate symbol spanning the underside of our kitchen table, whorls of red chalk creating stylized hearts and crosses that grew into the same image I'd seen carved into Erzulie's door.

The bundles of herbs and flowers hung over the windows, the bright sunlight fading the fragrant bundles to a brittle yellow until my mother replaced them with new herbs. The old bunches were tossed in the fireplace, filling the room with sweet, herbal smoke.

My father would smile even more than usual on those days. "My Creole witch is brewing something again," he'd say, tapping one of the fresh bundles, drawing out more of the sharp, green scent.

My mother would laugh and say something about how chemical air fresheners were toxic and wasn't this so much nicer. I never noticed how the smile never quite reached her eyes on those days.

The trips to the voodoo shops didn't end when I was a child, but I was included less and less. She would slide in behind the wheel of the Jeep, sunlight glinting off the glass beads of the carved wooden rosary that hung from the rearview mirror, and drive away, disappearing into the back rooms of the voodoo shops.

She avoided churches. Unlike most of my peers, I didn't spend my Sunday mornings in a droning Latin mass. Over the years a few baptisms or weddings demanded our presence, and she was always skittish and wary, the tense line of her shoulders belying the happy smile pasted across her lips.

"She's too young. It's too soon." She was sitting on the front stoop, the cordless phone pressed against her ear and lines of strain criss-crossing her face. Her voice was pitched low, hiding the discussion from my father. She never knew that I was sitting in the shadows by the open window. "I just want her to have a normal life for a bit longer. She deserves that."

They died a day later.

It's funny the things you remember.

"WHY WERE you so afraid of churches?" I wonder aloud, but the stones give no answer. "If we'd be safe anywhere I'd think it would be on holy ground."

"You would think that."

I freeze at the unfamiliar voice at my back, every part of me going cold.

"But she knew entering God's house would make her more visible to His soldiers."

I scramble to my feet, pressing myself against the back wall of the mausoleum. A man stands in the doorway, the fading light of the setting sun silhouetting him in a blaze of orange and gold.

The first thing I notice is his size. Lucifer is all compact muscles, his strength hidden from a casual glance, but this man – *angel,* my mind corrects absently – is built like a battering ram.

The grey suit he wears does little to conceal the thick muscles of his chest and arms. A build designed for brute force isn't made for a suit. While the inky fabric Lucifer clothes himself in flows around his form like a second skin, this one's jacket is ill-fitting, the seams fighting to contain him. His sandy blond hair is cut in a military crop, and his dark blue eyes briefly meet mine with a cold intensity of an assassin focusing on his target.

It has to be Michael. God's most fearsome warrior.

And I'm alone.

Michael seems to barely acknowledge my presence as he takes another step inside. His eyes sweep around the tomb, pausing on each name that catches his eye. "Arelia Celestin. She was a feisty one. Red hair and a mouth that would fit in more today than her time. It was 1921 when she died. That fire took out half the quarter. Her beloved husband Ducrest succumbed to the burns from the blaze a few days later."

"Genevieve was just 14 and only she made it out unscathed. We lost track of that one for far too long. This country was thick into a World War when she drowned in the Mississippi in '44. Her paramour Lacour went mad from grief and hung himself a month later, so dear sweet Rose was left to fend for herself."

Michael never pauses in his narrative as he moves closer to me, always blocking the door with his bulk.

"Rose was luckier than most at first. Her golden hair and sweet smiles caught the eye of a wealthy man. Sacriste owned half the ports in the city back then, but he wasn't loyal. When she told him of her family lineage, he tossed her in a madhouse and married again. Sweet Rose never stopped trying to get back to her daughter though, and she almost made it, but years in an asylum had sapped her strength. She lost her footing as she tried to climb through a window, shattering her body on the stones below."

"Serafine never stopped hating her father for what he had done to Rose. Her crafty mother had planned ahead though, leaving sheaves of papers with every word of the Celestin history written in her careful hand hidden with a trusted friend unknown to Sacriste. Your grandmother fled the city for the West. She met Anderson in California, and he was everything her father wasn't. She vowed never to come back, but New Orleans kept calling for her return. The power in this city called to her blood, so she packed up her family and made the long trek back."

I know who is coming next, and I want to scream at him to stop. I never want to hear their names cross his murdering lips, but Michael presses on as he takes another agonizingly slow step closer to me.

"Serafine was unique. She was the first to live long enough to see her grandchild born. You were just a tiny creature, the very image of her daughter when she was taken, but for one blissful year she believed that the curse had ended with you and with Marianne.

"As for Marianne and dear Will Murphy, I think you know what happened to them."

The thick glass vase on the ground by my feet shatters, sending shards of glass and wilting flowers flying. Michael quirks an eyebrow, looking slightly impressed. "So it's true then, you really are the Last. You would do well to come with me now."

"Like hell I am," I spit. I know I have little recourse against Michael, but there's no way I'm going to make it easy for him. "He knows where I am. He'll come for me," I bluff.

"No, he won't. Do you think Lucifer cares for you, child?"

Michael asks, his lip curling in a sneer at Lucifer's name. "I can smell his stink all over you. Do you think humanity matters to him at all? You're nothing but a tool to him. Something he can use and play with. He's the enemy here, not me."

Michael's words prick at the lingering doubts in the back of my mind about Lucifer's intentions with me, and I falter for just an instant. Michael notices and grabs my shoulder, preparing to drag me outside into the darkening cemetery.

I squeeze my eyes shut, bracing myself for a killing blow that never comes. Instead, I feel something buried so deeply within me that I never knew it existed awaken.

Fire courses through my veins, waking up senses and nerves dulled by generations of mortality. The glass cage that held me back shatters, and I just *know* what I need to do.

I push against Michael, a man who even without angelic strength easily outweighs me by a hundred and fifty pounds. He flies backward, his body impacting with the side of the mausoleum. A long crack splits the face of one of the graves, cutting Serafine's name in half.

I stare down at my hands in shock, the power coursing through them feeling like tiny insects crawling up my skin. I glance back at Michael. The blow dazed him, but I won't be lucky enough to surprise him twice.

I run.

Thankful for a city that values ambiance over modern convenience, I duck down one of the darkened thoroughfares into the cemetery. The only streetlights are by the main gate, but I spent my childhood walking among these stones. I don't need light to find the paths.

"You're making a mistake Grace!" Michael's voice echoes through the cemetery, far too close for comfort. His heavy boots crunch on the loose gravel as he searches for me, making no effort for silence, and I don't exactly disagree with his bravado. Those blazing bright streetlights mean making a stealthy exit is impossible.

Hopefully, Michael doesn't know about the back gate. Much less stately than the main entrance, the back gate is a half-forgotten door in the high iron fence used by caretakers and bored teenagers looking for a place to smoke pot at night.

Silently I pick my way through the rows of mausoleums. Michael has fallen silent, and my ears strain for any sign of him. My knees buckle under me and I clutch at the edge of a grave to keep from hitting the ground as my head swims. The stone creaks under my fingers as the pressure cracks the hundred-year-old marble.

I try to catch my breath, try to push down the forces tearing through my very cells. I bite my lip until I taste copper, all the while screaming *MOVE* inside my head.

A hand clamps over my mouth and yanks me back into the deeper darkness between two mausoleums. I struggle on reflex, trying to twist away from the grasping hands until a familiar voice hisses in my ear. "It's me. Be still."

Lucifer.

I sag against him, not even trying to hide the trembling that has nothing to do with fear or cold and everything to do with my body's realization that I'm something *other*.

I blink, and Lucifer has a blade in his hand. Long and thin and wickedly sharp, it glints in the faint streams of moonlight that filter to our hiding place. "Wait here," he mouths and takes a step back toward the path and Michael.

Another wave rushes over me, and I know that without the solid stone against my back I'd be on the ground. Before Lucifer can move any further away I grasp his wrist, digging my fingers into his arm and silently pleading him to not leave me.

Lucifer hesitates, glancing back at the path.

Sounding like he's only a few rows away, Michael's shouts reach us. "You're nothing to him, Grace! Lucifer will destroy you."

With an indecipherable look on his face at Michael's accusations, Lucifer stows his blade and helps me stand, half-carrying, half-dragging me through the labyrinth of graves and past the gate into the city.

"YOU COULD HAVE BEEN KILLED."

I expect him to yell. To roar and rail at me for risking his plan and forcing him to choose saving me over killing Michael. I expect anything but this.

His grip on my arm as he drags me through the deserted hotel lobby is strong enough to bruise, but I barely notice it. The traces of power crackle over my skin, heightening every sensation and making that rough touch feel like a caress.

For the first time in a very long time, I feel alive.

Lucifer pulls me through the door of the suite, slamming it behind us, plywood and metal giving the illusion of safety.

He abruptly releases my arm but makes no move to take a step back. His dark eyes bore into mine, seething with anger and something else I can't identify.

"You could have been killed," he repeats, and I realize just what that rage is masking.

Fear.

He's so close. Fallen or not, angels don't seem to quite understand the concept of personal space and the heady mix of my burgeoning abilities and his proximity has my head swimming. Heat radiates from his body, and I can smell the intoxicating scent that seems to come from his very skin, smoke and spice, something dark and forbidden.

Lucifer is still, his face cast in shadow. The bright neon

lights filtering in through the uncovered window offer the only illumination. My back against the wall and the *actual Devil* in front of me, but the only thing I feel is *safe*.

"He could have killed you," he breathes, the anger draining from him. He sounds desperate. Unsure. A far cry from the powerful creature that shattered half the windows on my street just by speaking.

His eyes dart down to my lips, just for an instant, and a jolt runs through me.

I don't know which of us moves first, but Lucifer's lips are on mine. The touch is bare, so subtle they hardly seem to brush my own, just the play of breath on flesh. My hand grips the front of his shirt, crushing the black fabric between my fingers as I urge him closer.

Lucifer surges forward, pressing me to the wall with his larger frame, and for once in my life, I stop overthinking. I follow the instincts that threw me down this insane rabbit hole of angels and demons.

Those instincts tell me to kiss him back as hard as I can.

He tastes like sin and power and everything I've ever wanted.

And far too quickly it's over.

He pulls back, just enough to break the contact between us. His breath ghosts over my lips, and I want more.

"Stay here," he says, his voice unreadable.

Then he's gone, the door slamming in his wake.

11

LUCIFER

I kissed her.

That's not the issue at hand though.

The desire to kiss those inviting pink lips of hers or to bury myself in her ripe, young body isn't what drives me from her arms and out into the streets of this gloriously hedonistic city.

I felt something.

I tore myself from Heaven and my place as my Father's favorite. I spent thousands of years buried in Hell and meting out torment to the souls strapped to my rack, bereft of my Father's love. Still, I felt nothing.

Until a breakable, human girl with Heaven in her blood crossed my path.

Not so breakable anymore though. Those last fetters of mortal weakness have shattered and the true glory of what she is surrounds her, overwhelming her still human mind with its intensity. It's intoxicating. *She* is intoxicating.

This will not do.

Friday night and choked with people, the streets echo with the revels of the tourists vying for space with the locals.

Their thick drawls fill the air with their eagerness to unwind after an exhausting week of enduring their small, human lives.

What am I doing?

I can still taste her. Innocence tempered with an iron strength that has very little to do with her newly awakened abilities.

And so much loneliness.

I don't need to read her soul to sense that.

It makes sense. Some unconscious part of her has always recognized the difference in her blood, and that hidden angelic nature kept the world at arm's length.

Some part of me recognizes you. . . knows you.

Her resolve didn't waver in the face of my true nature. It only drew her closer. I was the one to put the first crack in the wall holding her powers back, and she tore through the rest like a battering ram to finally free what she really is.

None of this should surprise me.

Every part of me aches to be closer to that taste of Heaven that surrounds her. I want to possess it- possess *her* until that delicious purity is as sullied as my own. And it would be so easy.

But the tiny shards of me that remember I was once an angel cringe at the thought. Grace is the uncorrupted memory of Heaven before my Father cast us out to survive alone.

She wasn't made for this world.

Even more, she wasn't made for *me*.

I glare upward at the night sky, the steel-grey clouds and faded stars showing no indication of the celestial world they hide.

"This is some cosmic, fucking joke to you, isn't it?" I snarl, barely knowing myself just who I'm yelling at. "You lock me in Hell for not adoring your precious humans enough, but I seem to be the only one left who gives a damn about this world."

I stand in the middle of the sidewalk, the fury pouring off me causing the masses to give me a wide berth. "You send her to me as what? A test?" The skies give no reply. "I'm not going to play your games," I spit. "Not anymore."

Someone brushes my shoulder, and I turn my attention on the mortal foolish enough to get too close.

Black eyes. Even blacker soul.

I can think of one thing to chase her taste from my mouth.

Blood.

"You'll do."

HIS EYES ARE BLACK, but beneath the mask of the Hellbound soul riding him, they are brown. His face and build are unremarkable. Even his clothing choices are forgettable, worn jeans and a faded grey sweatshirt. Everything on the surface is deceptively average.

Underneath though, that's where things get interesting.

The alley smells of spoiled food from the half-filled dumpsters, and it seems only fitting. The soul that has taken over this man is dark, but it pales in comparison to his own.

Like attracts like, after all.

Decay breeds even more rot.

Wrath. A short, skinny boy dropping to his knees as a fist impacts his stomach. The laughter of the crowd cutting off abruptly as he jams the jagged piece of glass into the popular boy's face.

Envy. Those happy faces, those adored children. Let them suffer as he has. If he can't have their lives, he'll take them.

Lust. The red pouring over his hands as he rends their soft, unmarred flesh. Their tears only make him harder.

Pride. He'll show them. He'll show them all.

I take a step back. The soul has already twined itself through this twisted psyche, making itself at home in an already blighted mind. Pulling them apart at this point will leave his own soul and mind in shreds as the hooks his guest has snared him with rip him apart.

No great loss there.

"The Devil made you do it then?" I mutter. "Of course. Why claim responsibility for your own choices when you can blame the monster in the closet." I press my hand against his clammy forehead, curling my lip in disgust at the images that flood me.

"Mommy never hugged you enough, so you decided to make your little corner of the world bleed."

He laughs. Slowly he tilts his head up, the black eyes focusing on my own. "I'm keeping this one." The voice slow and garbled as the soul forces unfamiliar vocal cords into speech. "I'm staying here inside this one."

"Like Hell you are." I push harder against his skull as the soul resists. A bright drop of blood trails from the man's nose, and a low, animal groan of pain comes from his lips as the soul digs its proverbial claws into him.

Even entrenched as this soul is, it has little chance of retaining its vessel against me. Blood pours from his nose as I snap its hold and send it plummeting down to my domain, tatters of its host's soul clenched in its non-corporeal fists.

Like a puppet with its strings cut, the man crumples to the ground, blood smeared across his face. His dull brown eyes stare unblinkingly at nothing.

He still lives, but the damage done is irreparable. He's nothing more than breathing meat now. Killing him would be a mercy.

I may be feeling many things today, but mercy is not one.

I step over the body and disappear back into the crowd.

I WALK FOR HOURS, navigating my way through side streets and alleyways without seeing them. I tell myself that I'm hunting Michael, that every step I take retraces his own and brings me inches closer to *finally* ending this.

It should come as no surprise that the Devil lies, even to himself.

I feel her, rising heat at the edge of my consciousness as she fights to rein in her new strength, and I know I need to return. A piercing note of fear cuts through the assault of sensation as her mind cries out for me.

It's too much for her. Her skin stretched too tight with the essence of Heaven, and she cries out for *me*.

And I want nothing more than to answer.

I notice my surroundings for the first time in hours, and I can't hold back the bitter laughter that wells up in me. The glass doors of The Saint gleam in front of me, beckoning me inside.

Lucifer will destroy you. The memory of Michael's sneering voice mocks me as I stare at those doors.

I am Lucifer. Prince of Lies. Lord of Hell. The Supreme Tempter of Mankind. And somewhere underneath the blood-soaked memories of Hell, I am still the Bringer of Light. The Morningstar. *His* favorite.

And I ache for that- for *her*.

I fucking hate prophecies.

I push open the door.

GRACE BARELY NOTICES when I enter the suite. She lays sprawled on the couch with her eyes closed, silent except for her ragged breathing. Her red dress is wrinkled and tangled around her thighs, and equal parts of me wants to shield her from the world and tear her clothes off.

I scarcely believe it's been only a day since we met.

"Lucifer," she says, pulling herself unsteadily to her feet. Her eyes are too bright, too unfocused at first, but she repeats "Lucifer" and takes another tentative step toward me.

"You must focus, Grace." I keep my voice low and even, knowing her raw nerves can't handle more than that. "You need to control this, or it will rip you apart." Grace whimpers, and I doubt she realizes the noise came from her. "The human body isn't meant to contain an angelic essence for long, let alone God's own bloodline. That's why the Nephilim always went mad in the end. Their minds couldn't endure the power flowing through them."

"I can't." Her voice is small, and she picks up one of the random decorations scattered around the room as a demonstration, a small bowl made of gilded glass. It splinters under her grip, a bright shard slicing open her palm.

I rush forward to grasp her hand, and everything freezes.

It's like completing a circuit when my hand touches hers. Her power roars through me, momentarily blinding me with pure white light, and I marvel that she hasn't gone nuclear yet. She could flatten a city block if she breaks, and she's so close to breaking. I have untold millennia of control under my belt, and I feel drunk on just this brief taste.

My eyes refocus, and I see the fear draining from her, her eyes clearing and her stance growing steadier. Her other hand reaches up to brush my cheek, and I catch it with my own, searching her gaze for the desperate madness of a few moments ago and seeing only clarity.

"Lucifer," she breathes, and the last cord of restraint snaps within me. It feels like freedom, like free will, and everything I forsook Heaven to experience. I surge forward, hauling Grace against me. She melts, falling into me like she was built for no other purpose than *this*. My hands and mouth are everywhere, tasting the hollow of her collarbone and the curve of her neck, the line of her jawbone and finally *finally* those ripe lips.

I kiss her with abandon, and she returns the fervor, her mouth wide and wet against my own, pouring every drop of herself into me. Hesitation and inhibitions forgotten, she holds nothing back, and some tiny half-dead crumb of a conscience that escaped the fires of Hell tries to warn me back. She might be stronger now physically, but there are still so many other ways to bleed.

I stay silent though, tamping down that ember of morality as Grace's hands trail down my chest. She fumbles with one of the fastenings of my shirt for a moment before impatience wins out and she tears it down the middle, tiny buttons scattering in every direction.

Her slender hands slip through the open folds of my shirt, shoving it and the jacket off my shoulders to the ground before breaking the kiss long enough to catch her breath.

We're both breathless already, and I've barely touched her, something I intend to rectify immediately. The two thin straps holding up her dress snap under my fingers, and she kicks away the crimson puddle of fabric that snares her feet as I yank her closer. Her skin smolders against mine, hotter than it should be as her body tries in vain to fight off her new nature, and her fingers claw at my back as though every cell in her body is screaming for her to get *closer*.

It is incendiary. I'm more than accustomed to having this effect on the mortals I chose to bed. My presence strips away their reserve, those desire killing hang-ups that tell them this wanton hunger is wrong and that the craving yearning *want* inside them is sin on par with murder or blasphemy. I've played thousands of bodies like instruments until their souls threatened to break under the onslaught of sensation, but I've never known how it felt from the other side.

Grace's touch threatens to consume me entirely as her mouth grazes my jawline, her movements showing a desperation that neither of us can put into words. I lift her up, and those long legs twine around my hips, pulling me against the center of her, her last secrets concealed by nothing more than a thin scrap of black lace.

I stumble to the bed and press her back into the king-sized mattress. Seeing her spread across those pale sheets, her body nearly *writhing* has my mind short-circuiting, some central processor overloading at this endless feedback loop of arousal we seemed caught in.

I kick off my shoes and shed my pants, no doubt tearing zippers and ripping fabric in the process and no part of me cares. The bed dips under my weight, and I skate my hands over her body, barely grazing the globes of her breasts, sliding across each rib before clutching her hipbones and pulling her upward to straddle my waist.

Her lips find mine in another searing kiss, and I want to map every inch of her, to memorize the topography of every dimple and curve, taste every freckle or scar. I shift underneath her, easing her off my lap and hissing at the momentary loss of contact. I'm nothing though, if not patient.

I slide off the edge of the bed, the plush rug flattening under my knees, and tug Grace closer, ripping off the tiny triangle of lace like an afterthought, leaving her spread out like a feast before me.

Heaven never made me kneel, but for a taste of her I'd gladly prostrate myself.

I kiss my way up each thigh, feeling them trembling beneath my lips as I hover so close to where she wants me. Her fingers tangle in my hair, the grip just painful enough to incite me more.

"Lucifer please!" she begs, her voice rough. I glance upward and see her staring down at me, lips swollen and pupils blown, the grey of her irises swallowed up by hunger, and I know I must look the same.

Never let it be said that the Devil can't be merciful when it suits him.

At the first touch of my tongue on her fevered flesh Grace arches off the bed, her hips rearing upward as I press deeper into her, tasting heat and musk until she's shaking. Her nails bite into my scalp, and a litany of *yes* and *more* and *now* pours from her lips.

When she comes apart beneath me, it isn't Heaven she cries out to. It's my name on her lips.

"Come here," she demands, her body still shuddering from my attentions. "No more teasing."

"No more," I echo, settling myself atop her, skin to skin, unbroken by clothing, by posturing, by the expectations of Heaven or Hell. If the world burns down around us tomorrow, whatever happened tonight was something real.

Her hand snakes between us, grasping my length and drawing me closer to her. I catch her lip between my teeth as I press against her heat, swallowing both our moans as I fill her with a single deep thrust.

Grace clings to me, fear of her new strength forgotten as she rakes her nails down my back, trying to force me to speed my movements.

I can't help smirking just a bit at her frustration, but still I take my time, drawing out every movement like this press of skin on skin is something worth savoring and not just another night's amusement.

Grace rolls her hips, and I finally relent in the delicious, torturous pace, sliding my hand underneath and lifting her up off the bed, thrusting deeper with a hard snap of my hips. I give Grace the taste of the Devil she's been craving since the first time I touched her, wild and forbidden, fearless with the knowledge that she isn't just another fragile human with skin that bruises and bones that shatter.

I set a new, devastating rhythm, fucking Grace until she knows nothing else — the hard perfect slide of my cock inside her, the stretch and heat of every shift. Everything else disappears.

Grace's hair is a tangled halo around her, and she kisses me. It's almost gentle, the press of her lips against mine, and it anchors us both to this world again, to something real and something worth fighting for.

I feel her clench around me, crying out as she shatters with a rough indecipherable yell wrenched from somewhere in the center of her being.

So close, and there is a moment where everything hangs still, heat and breath suspended heavy in the air, and I can feel myself- my *true* self- unfurl from inside this human form that I wear like another dark suit.

Like a star going supernova, I drag my own angelic pleasure through Grace. I know she can feel the tendrils of what I am now and what I once was pressing at her skin from every direction, weaving her together and tearing her apart with every pulse.

If she were fully human, the pleasure would kill her or drive her mad. But she isn't and it doesn't, and she just hangs on tighter as I spill within her, the shadows of my wings blocking out the growing light of the dawn, cocooning us in darkness for just a bit longer.

❧ 12 ❧

GRACE

I open my eyes and see bright white.

I blink, focusing on the wall a few feet away and seeing the tiny imperfections in the plaster with a sharp clarity that seems almost too real.

Then I notice the warm body pressed against my back and forget all about the walls.

Lucifer's arm is slung around my waist, and his hand presses against the curve of my hip, the touch feeling possessive and more than a little distracting. I shift and feel his grip tighten momentarily before relaxing.

"How do you feel?" His low voice murmurs in my ear, and I don't try to hide the shiver that goes through me.

The memories of the hours alone in this room drift over me, hazy as a fever dream. I paced, circling the spacious room like a penned in animal, the foreign sensations twisting through my body making me want to climb the walls like a strung-out junkie.

More than anything physical, the mental effects were terrifying. The droning buzz in my ears had slowly formed into words, thousands of garbled tongues speaking over each other in a dozen languages that turned into a relentless wall of sound that clamping my hands over my ears did nothing to dampen.

I lost track of time after that, collapsing onto the long white couch and trying desperately to will myself sane again, all the while repeating the mantra of *Lucifer Lucifer Lucifer* in my mind, begging for his return.

I thought he was another hallucination when he walked in, but once he touched my hand it all went silent. The fear and the pain drained away, replaced by Lucifer's iron control, and it was just him and I and our mutual desperate need to get closer.

Even now, we can't seem to keep from touching each other. Lucifer's fingers toy with the tangled mess of my hair, and I feel his breath on the back of my neck.

How did I feel? In the space of little more than a day, I discovered I'm the last in a line of cursed women that stretches all the way back to God's own daughter. Angels killed my parents and are still hunting me. I have actual supernatural powers. On top of all that, I've just had the best sex of several lifetimes with *the Devil*.

"Grace?" Lucifer prompts, drawing me back to the present.

I twist in his grip to face him. Reclined in the jumbled mess of white sheets, his dark hair tousled, Lucifer looks calm, but I can sense the almost immeasurable well of strength that surrounds him. And despite knowing who he is and what he's done for thousands of years, I feel no fear.

"I feel different," I say, my voice sounding altered to my ears. The hesitance is gone, the small quaver that always warns every female to stay quiet and not take up too much space in the world. I stare at Lucifer, and for the first time I can see beyond the handsome face he wears. I remember the wings surrounding us; their feathers burned the color of soot and ash. I don't need to ask if they'd been white once.

The girl who worked at a shitty bar with dead parents and too much student loan debt is gone, and the past few years already feel like a memory of someone else's life.

"I feel strong," I add, opening and closing my hand and feeling the muscles and tendons stretch and move with a level of awareness I've never known. "I feel awake. Ready. I'm not afraid anymore."

The old Grace was waiting for someone to rescue her. But as I watch Lucifer's lips curl into the grin that's rapidly becoming familiar to me, I realize that he and I might just save each other.

"READ HER SOUL."

The midday sun filters through the thick branches and glossy leaves of the magnolia tree above our heads. The honey-sweet perfume of the blossoms mixes with the scents of dark coffee and frying beignets in the square. Even surrounded by people, my mind keeps slipping back to the room we just left.

It took the better part of two hours for us to make it out of the suite. Lucifer pulled me into the shower with him, pressing my back against the cool glass as the water poured over our skin in torrents. His hands mapped every inch of my flesh under that warm spray, his mouth endlessly searching for mine as steam surrounded us.

"Mind wandering?"

I come back to the present, and my cheeks flush at the memory. Lucifer's dark eyes hold a glint of amusement at that. He knows exactly what I was thinking about.

"Not that I can blame you for being a bit. . . preoccupied," he drawls, one long finger idly tracing the back of my hand, the feather-light touch making me shiver. "But we need to figure out the extent of your abilities and how to control them." Lucifer sobers immediately, the teasing tone disappearing from his voice. "You were very very lucky with Michael last night. You caught him by surprise when your powers manifested, but he won't allow that to happen again. And if I hadn't found you when I did, I doubt it would have mattered."

Lucifer keeps his voice carefully measured as he talks about just how close I came to my own death last night, but I don't miss the flicker of *something* in his eyes at that admission. Neither of us are willing to name whatever is growing between us. Not yet. Maybe not ever.

"How did you find me?" I ask, remembering the overwhelming feeling of relief that flooded me when Lucifer found me hidden between the graves.

"My sigil. Your fondness for carrying around that coin lead me right to you. I doubt we'd need it now though," he adds, voicing the thought that has been nagging the back of my mind since I woke up beside him. "We're bound, you and I. I don't understand the intricacies of it myself, but it's there."

I nod. I can feel it too, an *awareness* of Lucifer that has nothing to do with the strength of the most powerful fallen angel that radiates from him. Instead, it feels like the warm press of sunlight across my skin, heat that can sustain you or burn you alive.

"Now," Lucifer says, the silken tone of his voice turning serious. "Read her soul."

Lucifer doesn't elaborate on just who I'm supposed to read, so I scan the crowd, discounting person after person until I pause on a woman in a cream-colored business suit staring at the screen of her phone with a bored expression. Somehow I just *know* she's the one Lucifer means.

I narrow my eyes, staring at her from across the square and try to see beyond the surface to pluck details from her soul with the ease Lucifer does. Slowly, images start to coalesce in my mind, and the whispers that Lucifer's presence had silenced awake.

I search for her sins, sifting through the details and images that threaten to flood me, ticking off *wrath* and *pride* and *lust* like a grocery list, but they stay insubstantial as smoke.

I shake my head. "It's just a jumble," I mutter, rubbing my eyes as though they're the problem. "I can see the sins, but it's like they're muted somehow."

Sighing, I try again, forcing my perception beyond the suit and the designer handbag, beyond the dark hair pulled back into a severe bun and the downturned slash of red of her painted lips. Her story is just that of another person out of billions, but to her it's everything.

Forgiveness. Sitting in the back of the basement room with a crowd of strangers, watching while her father accepted a chip announcing five years of sobriety and hugging the man who once terrified her.

Pride. But not for herself. For him overcoming his demons. It would have been easy to walk away, to keep hating him. Letting the hurt go took work, but it was worth it.

I feel Lucifer's touch on my arm, drawing me back from the woman's mind. I blink my eyes, the images of her life receding into something manageable.

"Her name is Tara." I speak haltingly, slowly sifting through everything I had seen. "Her father was an alcoholic. She was afraid of him when she was younger. She hated him then, but he turned his life around." I stop, remembering the glow that surrounded the memory of that basement room. "She was so proud of him. She forgave him."

"Forgiveness." Lucifer echoes. "Of course. You can see their virtues. And their sins are just dust and smoke to your eyes, aren't they?" Lucifer glances back at the woman, and I wonder if the good in her is something he sees as flimsy and half-hidden by sins and transgressions.

"Of course," he says again. "You are your Father's daughter after all. It's not surprising you can only see the good in them. It's a family trait." Lucifer does nothing to disguise the bitterness in his voice. He pulls his hand back from where it rests on my bare arm, and I can feel him shuttering himself against me as though I'm just another angel, toeing the line of holy obedience.

As though I don't still have the image of his wings burned into my memory with the same clarity as his touch.

"Lucifer." I lean across the small table that separates us, focusing on the sun-warmed iron under my hands to keep from reaching for him. "I'm not Michael. You couldn't corrupt a truly virtuous soul even if you wanted to, right? That means they exist, but that doesn't mean I'm going to turn into some holier than thou asshole who thinks humans are perfect." I settle back into my chair, warily gauging Lucifer's reaction as I add. "Considering what I've experienced from the hosts of Heaven, I'm a lot more inclined to side with Hell, whatever my abilities might be."

"Don't be so quick to throw away Heaven, Grace. You don't know what you're giving up."

"Then explain it to me." Lucifer doesn't reply at first. I sit back in my chair, the rickety iron creaking under my movement. The square around us teems with life - the raucous voices of vacationers who began the day with a few too many mimosas, the chatter of the street vendors hawking t-shirts and jewelry to anyone who walks by, the distant sound of horns as a jazz band tunes up a few streets over. It all fades into a faint background hum around us, discounted and forgotten.

"Tell me about it." I don't elaborate beyond that, unsure myself if I'm asking for the truth of Heaven or Hell.

Lucifer's muscles are rigid as he sits, his mouth stretched in a close-lipped smile that doesn't reach his eyes. "You want me to tell you about Heaven." His voice is flat, devoid of its usual animation and I instantly regret ripping open millennia old wounds, but the deed is already done. "You can't begin to understand it. Divine blood or not, it's not something that can be explained in words that your mind can process."

Lucifer tips his head back, the bright sun illuminating his features. His eyes close as he draws up memories he spent thousands of years repressing.

For me.

When he speaks again, his voice somehow sounds younger, lighter, as though the weight of his choices and punishment has eased for just an instant. "It was warmth. Comfort. Security. At least it was in the beginning." His face darkens, and it's like a cloud has blocked out the sun. "It was perfect, like being wrapped in a blanket of our Father's love, safe in the knowledge that we alone were first in that affection. But it wasn't free. Your kind came along, and I learned quickly enough that His love came at the price of complete obedience." Lucifer opens his eyes, fixing that dark gaze onto me. "That's the great cosmic joke of it all. My Father made me what I am. He gave me the will and the desire to wonder. To question. To say no."

Lucifer pinches the bridge of his nose, his face twisting into a pained grimace at his next words. "But however much I saw Heaven's flaws, it was all I knew. It was my home. Imagine being *ripped* from that and thrown into a prison of blood and pain and regret, and knowing, absolutely *knowing* that He was well aware of exactly what it would do to me. What it would turn me into."

Lucifer's breath catches, and I reach across the table without thinking, wanting to give him whatever comfort I have to offer. He tenses at that first touch before tightening his fingers around mine as he continues. "Hell is just a word to all but a few zealots now, but it's Heaven's dark mirror. I challenged my Father because I didn't believe humans were worthy of the favor He bestowed on them, so as punishment He tossed me down to spend eternity with the worst creatures humanity had to offer. I may have been Hell's warden, but that doesn't mean I wasn't in shackles too."

"But then how were you able to leave?"

Lucifer blinks, before letting out a bitter laugh. "Another one of Dad's great jokes. You can leave Hell anytime. You just have to believe you don't belong there anymore." Lucifer pulls his hands back from mine, drawing back into himself. "Some of the Fallen have been able to come and go since the beginning. Phenex is one. He never really belonged in Hell, and even he knows it. But I never could until Michael started his little project unless I was summoned. I guess I should thank him for that, at least right before I gut him."

"You don't have to go back," I say, giving voice to the question hovering at the edge of my mind. "Do you?"

Every part of Lucifer seems to deflate with the question. "I don't know. You'd think I'd have a better answer than that. Hell was a well-oiled machine when I left. The demons and the lower-level Fallen do most of the dirty work punishing the souls. I make an appearance with those that are a bit more. . . high profile." Something in Lucifer's voice changes as he pulls the mantle of torturer back on. "Mass shooters. Clinic bombers. Those that kill for the fun of it." His voice oozes contempt. "I made time for them. But I don't know if Hell will slip into entropy if I'm absent too long."

Lucifer shakes his head, looking disgusted at himself. "It's my kingdom. It's all that I have now. All that I am."

"It doesn't have to be."

My words hang in the air between us, and I can see him building up the walls between us higher, appalled at showing me the chinks in his armor. I can't blame him. It's much simpler to be the Devil, to ignore any emotion deeper than lust or fear and keep anything real locked away.

I certainly understand the impulse. I've cultivated it myself for years and the last twenty-four hours has peeled away the protective layers I've encased myself in, leaving my psyche one raw nerve. Every touch, every look seems magnified a thousand times as seven years of numbness thaws.

"It's easier, isn't it?" I ask, looking around the square, my eyes flitting from person to person, wishing that I could see what he sees for just a moment. "I get that. Believe me, I get that." I pause on a man in a business suit, gesturing wildly as he talks into a cell phone.

Charity. He was rich. Richer than one person needed to be. He'd grown up with every privilege handed to him, moved into the family business and made a veritable killing, and he gave most of it away. He was on the phone arguing with a contractor trying to cut corners on construction for the school he was funding.

So much good, but for so long I hadn't been able to see any of it.

I'd been lost. So lost I didn't even realized it until now.

"Grace."

Lucifer pulls me back to the here and now, and when I turn to him, the words tumble from me. "After my parents died-" *Were killed*, my brain corrects. *They didn't just die. HE killed them.* "After they were killed, everything changed. I don't mean that in the 'everything was different because they weren't here' way. I mean something changed in *me*."

I don't look at Lucifer, knowing that if I see pity for the

poor broken human from him, I won't be able to stand it. Instead, I develop a sudden fascination with the iron table-top, tracing my fingertips over the simple diamond pattern of the metalwork. "Once the first excruciating wave of the grief was gone, it was like someone flipped a switch inside me and everything just shut down. It wasn't just shock or loss. I was completely numb to everything and everyone."

I laugh soundlessly, nothing more than a puff of air that has nothing to do with humor. "I actually snuck into my Uncle's office to flip through his old psych textbooks because I was afraid I might be a sociopath. Though, I guess, afraid wasn't really the right word because it still wasn't enough to make me *care*."

I finally look up at Lucifer, his complete silence getting to be too much for me to stand, and far from studying me with pity, he looks like he understands. "I made the mistake of mentioning it to my guidance counselor, and I ended up in therapy for six weeks. After that, it just became a lot easier to smile and pretend that I was processing everything in a healthy manner." Scorn drips from my voice at that memory. I'd hated the weekly sessions I'd been forced into at the time, hated the exhausting act I'd had to put on to get out of them even more.

"I didn't understand it then, and I still don't, not really. It couldn't have just been grief. I was normal before. I was a person, and afterwards I was a shell. A shell that couldn't bring herself to care that she was a shell." The highs and lows of the last few hours have almost left me feeling hungover, emotional pathways that atrophied for so long finally springing back to life. And I may not know why, but I do know how.

Or who.

"The first time I felt anything real in seven years was when you kissed me."

"It makes sense." The surprise I expect at my admission isn't there. He understands. Even in this, he understands.

It may just prove that I'm even more screwed up than I originally thought, but the understanding of Hell sounds a lot more appealing than the judgment of Heaven.

"If it makes sense to you, please, share with the class."

"Walk with me." Without waiting for my agreement, Lucifer takes my hand and pulls me down the street, weaving through the crowds in the square.

"Where are we going?" I ask, speed-walking to try and keep up with his long strides.

"Nowhere," Lucifer replies, slowing his pace to match mine. "Everywhere." At my confused look, he continues. "Angels feel things differently than humans. Most are soldiers. Explaining human emotions to them is like trying to teach calculus to a dog. And then some of us feel far too much."

An impromptu art show has sprung up outside of one of the cafes. Dozens of brightly colored canvases line the street, abstract slashes of greens and blues morphing into a sketch of Bourbon Street and finally the swirling purple and black of the sky after a storm. Lucifer pauses, scrutinizing the last painting with the sudden surge of curiosity that seems to be fueling him.

And somehow my fingers are still twined with his.

"When your mother lived, you weren't the Last. The divinity in your blood was shared between the two of you. Whether she did it consciously or not, she shielded you. When she died, that protection was gone, and everything that had been dormant for your entire life rushed to the surface and blotted out who you had been."

"She would have liked this one," I whisper, thankful for the distraction of the paintings and the crowds and Lucifer's long fingers still laced through mine. I follow Lucifer to the edge of the exhibit where a lone painting hangs like an afterthought - an overgrown landscape of tall grasses and wildflowers dotting the green-gold grasses with spots of purple and orange. "She was protecting me. Is that what you're doing now? Is that why things feel real again?"

"Yes." A quick tug of his hand and I'm stumbling into Lucifer's chest, his free hand curling around my waist and pulling me flush against him. He releases my hand and brushes his fingertips across my forehead, twirling a few strands of hair around his finger. "I'm sure it has something to do with that damned prophecy."

My gaze drops to his lips. Is there anything about this man that isn't pure temptation? A cabbie lays on the horn a block ahead of us, the noise jolting me back to reality and out of the cocoon of Lucifer's presence. "Is any of this real? Is this bond just another way to control you from your father?"

Lucifer's hand tightens around my waist, his fingers digging into my hip as he says "No" with such vehemence that I can't doubt him. He takes a breath before adding, "I lost everything for free will, Grace. I don't manipulate. I don't force any actions onto anyone that they haven't already completed a thousand times in their hearts. Whatever *this* is, it's not an illusion or a spell. It's real."

Standing on my toes, I kiss him. There is no uncertainty when Lucifer kisses me back, his tongue sweeping over my lower lip as he draws me impossibly closer, Heaven and Hell forgotten for now.

LUCIFER KICKS OPEN THE DOOR, the whisper quiet hinges no match for the Devil. The door slams into the wall, the knob denting the plaster before closing with a soft click.

It has barely been two hours since we'd left the suite for my impromptu training session, but that doesn't stop the heat from pooling in me at his touch. And touch he does. Lucifer's hands are everywhere at once, skimming over my hips and rucking my dress up my thighs, crumpling the blue fabric that impedes him from his goal.

The back of my legs hit the edge of the couch, and gracefulness definitely is not one of my new abilities. Lucifer catches me, saving me from the indignity of ending up sprawled on my back. He lowers me to the long white couch with a surprising gentleness before pulling my sundress over my head with a look on his face that's almost reverent.

I don't want reverence. I don't want to be treated like something holy and breakable. I don't want to think of virtues and divine blood. I want to bite the forbidden fruit and taste the juices until they drip down my chin. After so many years of living in solitude and detachment, I want every messy emotion. Whether he will admit to it or not, some part of me knows Lucifer feels the same.

I want to show Lucifer that I'm not His.

I'm his.

Instead, I slither out from under him, grasping a handful of the dark fabric of his jacket and steering him down to the couch. Lucifer allows me to manhandle him, looks of amusement and hunger vying for dominance across his face as I take control. I smooth my hand over the wrinkled lapel, the fabric soft, no doubt made by someone expensive and Italian, before pushing it off his shoulders.

"Off. Now."

"Bossy. I like this," Lucifer says, stripping off the jacket and tossing it aside, waiting expectantly for my next move.

Since he's already ceremonially divested me of my dress, I'm left in nothing but a pair of skimpy white lace panties and a pair of black flats (because when you might have to run for your life from a murderous angel only an idiot wears heels). My hair hangs down in its usual mane of curls, alternately obscuring and revealing my breasts as I move. Lucifer's eyes track my movements as I kick off my shoes and settle onto his lap.

His hands go to my waist, the electricity that always crackles between us making me shiver as he touches my bare skin, but beyond those feather-light strokes, he is content to sit back and watch what I plan do.

"I always seem to end up naked before you."

Lucifer's eyes meet mine, and I can already see the molten red fire smoldering underneath the deep ebony of his irises. I wonder if I'm the first person to look at that burning gaze without a spark of fear.

"I have no complaints about that."

I laugh softly and shift forward, biting back a groan as his hardness presses against the heat pooling in my core. I kiss his neck, feeling the pulse flutter under my lips as he tilts his head back, baring his throat to me. I run one nail down the column of his neck to the second button on his shirt, pushing the little disc through the buttonhole to bare a bit more skin. My hand joins the other, making quick work of the shirt, pushing the black fabric aside to bare the smooth, strong planes of his chest and shoulders.

Like everything else about him, his body is pure temptation. The contours of his muscles look carved from marble, though the statues of angels I've seen never appear quite so debauched. I run my nails down his ribs, scratching just hard enough for him to feel it, the sliver of pain making his breath catch and his fingers tighten on my hips.

Harsh panting breaks the silence in the room as I tease the Devil, rocking my hips against his and drawing him into a kiss that leaves me breathless and shaking, this strange new bond between us letting me feel his reactions as an echo of my own.

I expect the arousal and possessive desire but not this

lightness. I feel his lips smile against mine, and this man, this angel that is feared and reviled by the world can hardly kiss me because he's smiling so hard.

He's been alone for so long. The thought creeps up unbidden, a pang at our shared suffering twisting through me before I tamp it down.

I squeak in surprise as Lucifer stands up, his hands cupping my ass while he steers me toward the bed. I twine my hands around his neck, trying to get impossibly closer as he kisses his way across my collarbone.

"And they say I'm the master torturer." His voice is a low rumble against my skin. My back hits the window a moment later, the heat of the day warming the glass that stretches from floor to ceiling against my skin. I push his open shirt off his shoulders, my mind idly registering that that it isn't black as I had thought. Instead, it's a deep, dark red. Then Lucifer presses the full length of his body against mine, pinning me to the glass, and I forget all about the shirt.

My hands find his shoulder blades, fingertips searching for some indication of the black wings I'd seen, my hips moving against his in the frantic quest for more friction, teasing forgotten. I gulp down air like I'm drowning, my nails clawing little crescent moons into his back that would draw blood on a human.

I hear the rip of fabric as mass-produced lace gives way under preternatural strength, leaving me bare before him.

"Oops," Lucifer says, sounding completely unrepentant.

I stand on my toes, curling my hand around the nape of his neck to pull him down for another searing kiss, teasing his mouth open and letting him swallow my moan as he cups my breast, his thumb tracing my nipple and drawing out the heady noise of my pleasure.

"How do you do this to me?" he breathes, pulling back just far enough to speak before claiming my lips again.

I wiggle my free hand between our bodies, impressing myself that I manage to keep my hand steady enough to unfasten Lucifer's pants and reach inside, grasping his length in my hand, stroking him slowly to the sound of his ragged breathing.

With a dainty little jump, I wrap my legs around Lucifer's hips, my heels pressing into the backs of his thighs and urging him closer. For the first time, I appreciate my diminutive height. Pinned against the glass, Lucifer holds me like I weigh nothing, and when he presses inside me, filling me achingly slowly, I forget about our pasts and the dangers bearing down on us.

There is just this – the slick slide of his cock inside me, the unbroken press of skin on skin while the sun beats down upon us. A dozen stories up, but it isn't the altitude that has me feeling like I'm flying.

Every slow, measured thrust buries that lost, broken girl I'd been a bit more. Michael's attack might have awoken my powers, but it's Lucifer that's awaking *me*.

"Grace." Lucifer murmurs my name against my lips, so low I doubt if he even realizes he's speaking. When I cry out a few moments later, shuddering against him with my release, he holds me tighter, his grip almost bruising as he comes with a muffled curse.

It takes several long moments for us to come back to ourselves. Lucifer steps back, one of his hands sliding around my back, holding me flush against him once the support of the wall is gone. A few shaky steps and we're sprawled on the giant bed in a tangle of soft white sheets, curled around each other.

13

LUCIFER

I want to stay.

I feel the power of the bond between us growing, coiling through us both like the kudzu that chokes the countryside, twining its way through our thoughts and emotions with a strength that should make me feel caged.

Instead, it makes me feel free. When I reach out toward her with my mind, I feel the warm pulse of her soul, so different than the physical presence of her body pressing against my back. It feels like flying, like that first moment of unfurling my wings, the wind catching flight feathers and carrying me aloft. In those precious seconds, it all slips away – Heaven, Hell, innumerable centuries of blood and torture and regret. It's just the air rushing over my body and the heat of the sun on my feathers. It's light and freedom and everything I ached for in those early days before the Fall.

All wrapped up in her.

I suppose I should thank Michael.

That's the kind of thanks you give in person.

Grace wakes from her light doze as I'm dressing, the sun

just beginning to dip below the horizon. "Where are you going?" she asks.

"Where do you think?"

The relaxed line of her body instantly changes, going tense as she replies, "You're going to look for Michael."

I nod, and she moves to rise from bed. "I'm going with you."

"No," I say with a finality that actually makes her pause. "You aren't ready to face him yet." When she starts to protest, I cut her off. "Grace, this isn't something that's up for debate. I'm well aware of my own abilities and limitations, but I cannot hope to win a fight against my brother if I'm worried about keeping you safe as well."

I fall silent, watching her sit back down onto the bed, her emotions warring on her face. She wants to argue, wants to demand I bring her along instead of leaving her cloistered in this hotel like a princess in a tower. This princess wants to slay the dragon too, but despite her idealistic desire to be of use, her brain knows that she isn't ready to go toe to toe with an Archangel.

Reluctantly, she nods, but not before helping herself to fistful of my shirt, pulling me down to meet her lips in a kiss that turns hungry and greedy far more quickly than either of us expects, and it takes every inch of my self control to tear myself away from her.

Tonight, my brother is going to *bleed*.

EARLY EVENING, and Bourbon is no doubt choked with the usual crowd of revelers and laborers, the pickpockets and escorts weaving their way through the "upstanding" citizens.

I know Michael well enough that he won't be in the midst of anything resembling a crowd. Michael never was much for collateral damage, and his own twisted moral code will likely keep him from wanting to see the hideous outcome of his actions. Watching the city burn won't be nearly as much fun for him if he can't find a way to blame the blaze on me.

Instead, I head toward the parts of the city the rest of the country forgot about. The Lower Ninth Ward is still largely vacant, even a dozen years after Katrina ripped through. Vacant lots and houses that are little more than rotted skeletons line both sides of the streets. Of the structures that still stand well enough to be called houses, barely one in four looks inhabited.

An over-turned tricycle sticks out through the grass of the house in front of me, the deflated tire half buried by a decade of storms, bright metal and plastic faded to a dull shade of grey. The front door hangs crookedly, the rusted nails having worked themselves free of the rotting wood.

And of course, my brother chooses to lay in wait here.

I yank open the door, the weakened metal of the other hinges splitting under my touch, and I let it fall to the porch behind me, dried wood splitting on impact and filling the air with the musty smell of mildew and decay. Michael would have felt my presence the same moment I sensed him, so there isn't any point in trying for stealth.

And I do so like to make an entrance.

Standing in the middle of the gutted structure that was once someone's pride and joy is my errant brother. His blade remains undrawn, but I don't think for a moment that means he's unarmed.

Michael doesn't move during my scrutiny, sizing me up as I do the same to him. Centuries have passed, and empires have risen and fallen since the last time we stood this close to each other.

It didn't end particularly well back then, either.

Michael wears an ill-fitting tan suit, the seams stretching

across his muscular shoulders. I almost have to laugh at how uncomfortable he looks. My brother is made to wear armor, and his current choice of attire has him looking more like a personal trainer with a court date instead of the warrior he is.

I quickly forget that moment of levity when Michael speaks.

"I knew you were filth, Lucifer, but preying on *her* to make your realm stronger is low, even for you."

Unexpected fury pours over me when he mentions Grace, and I rush Michael. Expecting the usual barbs and posturing from me, Michael is unprepared for my sudden attack and my first punch throws him through a wall, the half-rotted studs and desiccated drywall crumbling under the force.

Michael climbs back to his feet an instant later, feinting to the right and catching me with a hard blow to my ribs. I feel the bones crack under his fist and I roll my shoulders, shaking off the twinge of pain as the bloodlust of battle seeps into me.

It's been far too long since I fought someone who is my equal.

I grab the back of Michael's neck, his close-cropped hair impossible to grip, so I dig my fingers into the base of his skull, driving him downward to slam his face into my knee. I hear the crack of bone, and Michael punches wildly, a jab catching me in my stomach.

Michael's broken nose streams blood as he backs up, keeping a few feet between us as a look that can only be described as familial irritation crosses his face. "Are you done?" he snaps.

"Hardly," I reply, striking out at Michael with an uppercut that would snap a human's neck if it had connected. Michael expects the punch this time, dancing back just enough so that my fist barely grazes the edge of his jaw.

"The girl belongs to Heaven, Lucifer. Her soul is not yours to corrupt."

"Since when have you cared about protecting any humans from my *corrupting influence*," I scoff, contempt dripping from my voice. "You'd do anything to wrest power from me. Every soul you trap here out of spite is corrupting another innocent, but apparently that's worth it to you!"

Michael's face fills with a look of such incredulity it's almost comical. "You think I did this?" he stammers. "Lucifer, I'm here to put a stop to it!"

The shock on his face almost makes me believe him.

Almost.

Michael never was a very good liar, but a few millennia will change anyone. Slowly, I unsheathe my blade, determined to end this once and for all. Michael backs up, moving us further into the small house.

The back door has long since rotted away, and the windows are nothing but black voids, the glass having been shattered by storms and bored teenagers years ago leaving no place to hide. I pause in the doorway to what was once a kitchen, a filthy refrigerator tipped on its side taking up half the floor space of the cramped room.

"Running away, Michael? I didn't expect that of you," I taunt, stepping through the doorway.

I hear the crack as Michael punches through the load-bearing wall an instant before the shower of plaster and wood hits me, knocking me to the ground. Already weakened by a decade of storms and neglect, it doesn't take much to bring half the roof down on top of me.

I struggle out from under the rubble, moldering insulation and drywall dust clinging to my body. I kick aside a sheet of curled tar from the roof, most of the shingles having long since blown off into the Mississippi.

Michael is gone.

"WHAT THE HELL HAPPENED?"

When I drag myself back through the door of the suite, the only thing I want is a shower and a strong drink. The dust and dirt from the house clings to my clothes and skin, turning my suit the color of a moldering corpse.

And Michael got away.

Grace is on her feet instantly, worry washing over her face as she runs her fingers lightly over the dried blood on my temple, the cut having long since healed. "Are you okay?"

I open my mouth to toss out some quip about immortality, but the look on Grace's face makes me reconsider my words.

Her fingers are still lightly pressed against my temple, reassuring herself that I'm unharmed. The look of concern on her face is so genuine I'm taken aback. Needless as it is, no one has ever concerned themselves with my wellbeing. I incite fear or hatred on a bad day, intrigue or desire on a good, but never something as simple as caring.

I smell like a musty basement and I'm fairly certain I have cobwebs in my hair, but that doesn't stop Grace from scanning me for any other injuries I might be concealing.

"I'm fine," I say, catching her fingers in my own and drawing them to my lips. "Immortal, remember? It'll take a lot more than that to end me."

Grace relaxes, the last threads of tension releasing their hold on her. Clad in one of those overly fluffy hotel bathrobes, she's swallowed up by the yards of white terrycloth. When she pulls back, the front is streaked with dust from my jacket.

"So I'm guessing you ran into Michael?"

I stalk over to the bar, pouring Grace a glass of whiskey before making one for myself. "Very astute," I drawl, yanking off my filthy jacket and tossing it over a chair before wandering to the wall of windows, staring out over the bright lights below us.

"What happened?" Grace prods, standing just close enough to me that the proximity crackles between us.

"We traded insults and then punches. I knocked him through a wall, he pulled the roof down on me and ran off." I can see just the faintest hint of my reflection in the window as I sip the smoky liquor. Grace's hand hovers over my shoulder, hesitating just for an instant before touching me. "I should have known Michael wouldn't make it easy."

Nothing has ever been easy. Why should it start now?

I WAKE hours later with the scent of her surrounding me.

Her face presses into the crook of my neck, that wild mane of hair falling around us like a curtain. She shifts in her sleep, rolling onto her back, and the pale sheet slips down, baring the creamy flesh I spent the night worshipping with my lips, whispering words in long-dead tongues into her skin.

Lust has never been my favorite of the seven deadlies. Not to say that I don't partake in more than my fair share, but I never threw myself into the endless train of flesh the way some of my Fallen brethren choose to.

Phenex seeks pleasure for its own sake, trying to slake his longing for Heaven in the body of whatever pretty creature strikes his fancy. Others like Asmodeus use desire as a weapon, drowning his hapless victims in lust until their own base needs drive them mad.

For myself, it's just another sensation. Another amusement and another cosmic fuck off to dear old Dad. Serve the humans? Let them give service to me instead.

The church always did like to say that the most powerful position is on your knees.

Bow down and worship then.

Somehow, this is different.

I look down at this girl, soft skin and lush curves spread out before me, and I *feel*.

Affection. Ease. The need to protect.

And something more. Something I haven't felt since long before the Fall in a time when my name was not synonymous with betrayal and evil. Something I can't bring myself to name, even in my own head.

"Lucifer?" Her voice is still thick with sleep, her eyes half open as she looks up at me.

"Rest," I murmur, the gentleness in my voice shocking me.

She smiles and settles back against me, her eyes slipping shut as sleep reclaims her.

Had I ever been so open? So trusting?

I search the dark recesses of my memories, long before Hell and the Fall, before humanity spread across the world to the forgotten days when me and mine were first in God's love. But even in those blissful days, I always ached for a choice.

Free will has been my curse from the beginning.

History calls it pride, but all I ever longed for was the chance to choose.

And here she is, throwing herself headlong into that same choice. Offering to toss her lot in with Hell without realizing the true weight of that decision and the folly of making it for vengeance.

Or for me.

. . .you aren't strong enough to stop him. . .

That witch's damned prophecy still hangs over our heads,

tangled up with the next inevitable confrontation with Michael.

I need answers. And I know just who to pry them from.

Carefully, I extricate myself from Grace's sleeping embrace, unable to help the slight smile that crosses my lips when her hand absently moves across the mattress, searching for me for a moment before drifting back into slumber.

Grace's clothing and my own is strewn across the floor of the suite, a messy breadcrumb path starting just inside the doorway. A lone black shoe peeks out from underneath an end table, while another one of the interminable sundresses she wears drapes over the back of the couch. My lips quirk as I remember peeling the sapphire blue fabric over her head earlier.

I glance back at the bed where Grace sleeps soundly. It would be so easy to crawl back beside her and lose myself in her skin for a few hours or days. To let Michael win. To let the world burn to ashes outside this room.

Didn't I deserve that for once?

Shaking my head at my own foolishness, I dress silently. Once I have Michael's head on a spike, I'll celebrate by locking myself in this room with Grace for a few days. . . weeks. I have more than a few pleasurable ideas to test the burgeoning power of the bond that links us together.

A flash of red catches my eye, peeking out from between the couch cushions. When I tug it free I see the red flannel mojo bag, the iron coin tucked inside, and I smile when I recognize it. I told her the bond between us made the coin unnecessary, but she still carries it around like a child with a security blanket, tracing my sigil with her fingertips and carving herself just a bit deeper into me with each circuit.

A stain darkens the edge of the fabric, the deeper red line that bisects the bag too precise to be accidental. I pull on the side, the flimsy stitches giving way easily. A bare-bones version of Erzulie's veve is painted on the inside of the bag, leaving the fabric stiff and brittle. I run my finger over the "paint" and feel the echo of the artist.

Blood. Of course. It's always blood.

I drop the coin soundlessly onto the coffee table and walk out.

***

SHE ISN'T difficult to find.

The door to her shop is unremarkable, at least for New Orleans. The veve carved into the door stands out starkly against the neat coat of yellow paint, the whorls and crosses that make up the symbol looking exotic enough to entice tourists to hand over their cash in the hopes of an "authentic voodoo experience."

Even a loa has to make a living, after all.

A more prudent man would enter quietly, taking the chance to observe her before she becomes aware of my presence. In the past, I would have partaken of that devilish subtlety I'm so famous for.

But my patience with prophecies and spells and all their related bullshit has long since worn thin.

One well-placed kick sends the door flying open, slamming back against a cabinet of cheap pottery she's hawking to tourists. Two women are inside picking through a rack of jewelry, the shorter of the two nattering on in a flat Midwestern drone about zombie tours.

"Out," I snarl, and they drop the glittering trinkets and run, the paste gems and tarnished silver scattering across the countertop.

Erzulie stands silently behind the counter, her youthful face carefully blank. Idly I wonder just how much I'd need to tear apart in this little shop to get an expression on that stony face.

"Tell me," I drawl, pressing both my hands against the countertop and leaning forward to scrutinize her. "Which is your real face? This one or the old woman?"

"Which is your true face?" she counters.

"Perhaps you'd like to take a look. I'm quite curious to see what would happen to you."

"You don't frighten me." She moves to turn away from me like I'm a petulant child throwing a tantrum.

Enough. Before she can blink, my hand is tightening around her throat. A few jars of herbs tip and shatter on the floor as I jerk her forward, filling the room with a sharp, dry scent. "The prophecy. Explain. Before I *rip* it out of you."

Erzulie wraps a slender hand around my wrist, shoving me back and standing up, her eyes flashing with irritation.

Not fear. In that moment, I almost like her.

She rounds the counter, yards of blood-colored silk swirling around her feet. She steps delicately over the broken jars littering the floor and leads me through a beaded curtain into the back room.

She sits at a small table draped with red and gold, motioning for me to take the other chair. "I thought a loa would be more than a two bit fortune teller," I scoff.

She ignores me, unwinding a square of leather worn smooth and thin as fabric to reveal a worn deck of playing cards. Silently she lays out five cards.

Ten of Spades. Seven of Spades. Nine of Clubs. Nine of Hearts. Jack of Clubs.

"It's always the same." Erzulie's finger rests on the Jack of Clubs. Her voice is low, and I can hear the old woman behind the youthful tones, gravel worn smooth by the tides. "Your journey. My warning. His betrayal. Her love. Her sacrifice." She ticks off each card with no more concern for her words than for the overblown fortunes of love and riches she peddles to tourists. And why should she be concerned? Prophecies are inevitable, as immutable as the seasons. She's only the messenger, after all.

Her sacrifice.

No. Not her sacrifice. Never her.

My denial must have shown on my face. She softens, the cold iron of her eyes turning to liquid amber. "You know what the Last means, Lucifer. It means there isn't another." She sweeps the cards back into the deck, her long fingers shuffling them deftly before pulling five cards again, laying them out before me.

Ten of Spades. Seven of Spades. Nine of Clubs. Nine of Hearts. Jack of Clubs.

"I've read them a hundred times." She moves to pick them up again, but I pluck the Jack of Clubs from the table, staring at the aged white card between my fingertips – faded paper and ink telling me that she is supposed to *die.*

"Sacrifice runs in her family, after all," Erzulie says, taking the card from my fingertips and adding it to the pile. "I think you already know that."

"What is she sacrificing herself *for?*" I demand. Not that dear old Dad ever actually needs a reason. "No more riddles, Erzulie. I had enough of that in the Bronze Age."

Her hands still on the stack of cards, and the barest smile crosses her lips, wistful and almost sad. "Redemption doesn't always have to be asked for, Lucifer." The room is quiet, the sound of the guttering candles the only noise breaking the silence.

I know what she's implying, but I refuse to believe it until the words cross her lips.

She nods slowly in understanding. "You don't need me to tell you what her sacrifice is for. You felt it the first time you touched her."

I stand up, backing away from the table, from the honey-sweet perfume of the candles and the thick, cloying scent of the incense. Away from those dark eyes that stare at me like I'm something to be pitied and not an Archangel that could reduce her to a stain on the floor without breaking a sweat.

I shake my head and mouth the word *no* because denial swallows up my voice. I want to tell her to hold her tongue because naming something gives it life.

"Her sacrifice is for you."

Interlude
Phenex

"What do you want, Fallen?"

Phenex saunters into the dilapidated house, wrinkling his nose in disgust at the remnants of water-stained plaster clinging to the skeleton of two-by-fours and the scent of decay hanging in the air. Most of the house has been gutted, rotted carpet and mildewed drywall having long since been removed.

If Heaven's greatest warrior chooses to bunk down here, it almost gives Phenex second thoughts.

Almost.

"Lovely accommodations, Michael," he says with disdain. "Just because you're an angel doesn't mean you have to scour yourself and sleep in shit like a bloody penitent."

Michael glowers. He never did have a sense of humor. His hand moves for the blade that's never far from his reach, taking a menacing step closer like a big cat stalking his prey.

"Temper temper. Don't you want to know why I'm here? It's certainly not for the ambiance. Or the company."

Michael ignores Phenex's words as he draws his blade, the razor-honed edge glinting faintly in the dim light.

Keeping his back to the door for a possible hasty retreat, Phenex blurts out, "I know where the girl is."

Michael lowers the blade, but still holds it at the ready. "And in exchange?" he demands.

"I want back into Heaven. And leave Lucifer out of it."

Michael stands still, regarding Phenex like an insignificant insect. He doesn't particularly expect honor between Hell's denizens, but such blatant treachery makes his annoyance at Heaven's petty squabbles fade.

Still, this might be the only way.

And how much honor is there in a promise to a Fallen anyway?

Closing the distance between them, Michael grasps Phenex's hand, striking the deal.

☙ 14 ❧

GRACE

The sheets are cold when I open my eyes.

I roll over, searching for the familiar presence of Lucifer beside me, wakefulness washing over me when I realize I'm alone.

I glance around the room quickly, seeing the clothes strewn about like a hurricane from last night, unable to keep the smile off my lips as I remember what had come next.

Lucifer isn't exactly the type to leave a note, so I decide to do a little recon of my own. Beyond breaking into my house and skulking around my family's mausoleum, I don't have any idea where Michael might be, but it's impossible to forget the damage I saw that human possessed with a tainted soul cause the day Lucifer and I met.

In the days of social media and 24-hour news networks looking to fill the hours, chaos like that always leaves a trail.

I flick on the television, turning it to a local station as I dig my laptop out of the depths of my suitcase.

"*. . .vandalism and brutal random attacks on the rise. Authorities suspect a new gang is terrorizing the city. We have exclusive footage* *shot from the victim's dash cam. Please be warned; this footage is graphic."*

I look up to see the grainy video of a man getting pulled out of his car by two others and dragged to the edge of the frame. Only his legs and feet are in view, and they thrash as he tries to fight off whoever (*whatever*) is pinning him down. A guttural scream rips from his throat before it cuts off abruptly, a large red stain growing beneath him. One of the assailants looks up, and even with the low resolution of the footage, it's easy to see the pure black of his eyes.

The scene switches back to the reporter, an artful look of concern across her blandly perky morning show face. *"Suspects are considered armed and extremely dangerous, and authorities warn citizens not to approach anyone involved with this gang."* The reporter's demeanor shifts as she smiles, revealing a row of perfectly capped teeth. *"And now we have Mike with the weather!"*

Punching the off button, I silence the inane chatter, my desire for background noise overridden by my annoyance at the news anchor's *"business as usual"* attitude.

Of course, a few days ago I would have done the same. Maybe I would have added a second deadbolt to my front door and shelled out the money to park a little closer to the bar at night, but I would have written off the weird occurrences just like everyone else. Gangs. Drugs. Mental illness.

I turn my attention to my laptop, scrolling through a local blog I follow.

HAS THE CITY GONE CRAZY?

The headline blares from the top of the screen.

New Orleans is always a wild place. Very few move here looking for a sedate lifestyle, but in the last week, our city has been under attack.

The cable news channels were quick to blame the sudden spike in violent attacks on a new gang moving into the area, but more recent reports show that most perpetrators are long-time residents with no history of violence or criminal activity.

I scroll down to the comments section, something that's rarely a good idea on any post, to see hundreds of replies.

I was walking home from Bourbon last night and saw a guy in a business suit beating the shit out of a homeless guy. It's definitely not gangs.

Zombie apocalypse. We all thought it would start in Florida. . .

Something in the water making everyone go batshit?

Obviously, this is all due to the lack of adequate mental health care in this country!

God is punishing your city for its depravity.

A few comments have photos or videos attached, and it's more of the same - unnatural strength, vicious, violent rage that comes from nowhere, and those cold black eyes. The reports are all over the city, stretching out into Metairie and beyond with no rhyme or reason to the locations, no pattern that I can see except the obvious.

It's spreading.

I hear the soft electronic click as the door unlocks, and I turn away from the computer to watch Lucifer stride into the room, his long legs taking him to the makeshift bar where he pours himself a generous splash of whiskey, tossing it back without looking at me.

I shiver, and it has nothing to do with the overly air-conditioned room and everything to do with the tense line of his shoulders as he stands with his back to me.

"Lucifer?" My voice sounds tentative, that faint little quaver that I thought I buried clawing to the surface.

"I have news." He turns to me, his face a mask. Cold. Impassive. His eyes bore into my own, the absent warmth turning them into two black pits.

Our short time together has educated me on the volatility of Lucifer's moods, but everything about him feels wrong. Yet my hands still itch with the desire to touch him, the bond between us tugging me closer like a gravitational pull – inevitable and unstoppable.

I know he feels it too, but he shrugs it off, keeping a few feet of distance between us. "The prophecy," he continues, his voice faltering so slightly that I almost think I'm imagining it. "I paid a visit to our mutual acquaintance." He refills the whiskey glass a second time but makes no move to drink the dark brown liquor.

"I'm the one meant to destroy Michael, not you." He gestures at the room with the glass, a few drops spilling unnoticed over the side. "This is all just a distraction. A bit of shore leave." He smirks and takes a step closer to me, and my traitorous body still wants to welcome him.

The first cold thread of fear slices through me as he stalks closer. I jump up from the couch, backing away from him slowly. His head cocks to the side, and my mind races through reasons of why Lucifer has suddenly turned into the heartless, bitter creature he swore not to be. "Why are you acting like this?"

Lucifer chuckles, and I wonder if that's the same laugh the souls hear strapped to his rack. "Why am I acting like this?" he parrots, the flat tone of his voice giving way to a quiet mockery. "This is who I am, Grace. You were kidding yourself to think otherwise. After all, what better way is there to stick it to my father than *sticking it* to his last descendant in this godforsaken world?"

He drains the glass of whiskey, clutching the empty tumbler with his fingertips as he shadows my movements. I don't even realize I've been steadily backing away from him until my back hits the unyielding glass of the window. Lucifer presses against me, pinning me to the window with lean, hard muscle. His free hand cards through my hair, pulling it back to bare my throat. "Fancy another round?" he breathes against my skin.

It takes everything in me to muster up the strength push him back, my body humming at his proximity even as my mind recoils from his harsh words. "Get out."

He stands in front of me, still holding me against the wall of glass with his sheer presence, and the tightly coiled rage radiates off him like body heat. Some small, self-destructive part of me wants to goad him into putting an angelic fist through the window, shattering the glass and sending us both plummeting to the crowded streets below.

Of course, only one of us has wings.

But an even smaller part of me, that desperately lonely girl who thought she had finally *finally* found a home is the one that speaks up. "I thought you-" the words tumble out of my mouth before I can stop myself.

Lucifer takes a step back, his hands dropping to his sides. For a moment he's still before he turns and throws the glass into the fireplace, the heavy crystal tumbler shattering against the iron grate.

"You thought what? That I loved you?" His face twists into a sneer as he practically spits out the word *love*. "I'm the Devil." He walks away from me, standing in front of the unlit fireplace and staring unseeingly into the hearth. "I lit the stars. I started a war that changed the face of existence. I've spent more years torturing souls than you can comprehend. I'm not some teenaged boy lead around by his cock."

I don't move. Still rooted to the spot, I wait to see where his mercurial mood is going to take him next as the familiar numbness pours over me.

How had I been so stupid?

Lucifer looks up, his eyes raking over my body in a way that has nothing to do with desire and everything to do with putting me in my place.

"Do you know the last time I loved anyone, Grace?" His voice is barely above a whisper, and I have to strain to hear him. The last words hit me with the same force as a silenced bullet. "The last person I loved was God, and you know how well that worked out for me."

I slide down the window, my rubbery legs finally giving out underneath me, and I sink to the floor. Lucifer strides to the door without looking back at me. He pauses with his hand on the doorknob.

"I don't know what else you expected from this. I am the Devil, after all."

❧ 15 ❧

LUCIFER

I close the door behind me with a soft click that sounds more final than a deafening slam, willing myself not to look back at her stricken face.

I slump against the door, the coolness of the smooth white wood seeping through my jacket as the mask crumples.

What have I done?

Every noise is muffled. The soft hiss of the air conditioner, the ding of the elevator door opening. The despair threatens to drown me, and I don't know if it's hers or my own.

What have I done?

I straighten, drawing myself up to my full height and step away from the door, tamping down on the bond that threatens to yank me back to her like a rubber band stretched too tight.

What have I done?

Probably the only unselfish act of my entire life.

I saved her from myself.

The elevator doors open, and I step into the shiny silver box, pushing the key for the ground floor. Steeling myself to be the unfeeling general again, I still keep my eyes on the closed door to the room, *our* room, as the elevator doors slide shut.

Forgive me.

PHENEX WAITS AT THE BAR, sipping something red out of a champagne flute and looking immensely proud of himself. His smile falters for a moment when he sees me, millennia of familiarity giving him a bit more insight than most.

"You look like you could use a drink," he says, sliding back into his usual jovial mood without missing a beat. "This city really is delightful. They have an entire bar menu based on the seven deadlies." He takes a long sip of the cocktail. "This one's Lust."

My jaw tightens, and only the awareness that if I drop my control for an instant, I'll never be able to rein it in again keeps me from backhanding Phenex. Right now the world can bleed for all I care.

As long as Michael bleeds first.

Seeing that I'm not in the mood for games, Phenex drops the act. "I found Michael."

"And you didn't lead with that?" I grind out.

Phenex shrugs. "He's not going anywhere. He's holed up in another one of the Katrina houses licking his wounds. I mean, bested by you and a human in the same day? God's most fearsome warrior isn't exactly inspiring much lately."

I crack my knuckles. Violence is just what I want right now, and it won't come from a blade. I want to feel Michael's flesh rend under my hands until I taste the iron in the air.

It must show on my face. Phenex rises from his chair, abandoning the ridiculous cocktail and falls into step beside me, but he keeps far more distance than usual.

Phenex glances at the bank of elevators in the lobby,

opening and closing his mouth quickly as he thinks better of his query.

Good.

I don't want to hear her name crossing his lips. Murdering the closest thing I have to a friend would be the perfect end to this miserable day.

"Take me to him."

MICHAEL IS WAITING. In a battered armchair mottled with dust and claw marks from stray cats sits my brother, his blade resting across his lap as he counts down the minutes until our arrival.

I should have seen it coming. A few days ago, I *would* have seen it coming.

Phenex, at least, has the decency to look guilty. He stops in the doorway, letting himself have the illusion of maintaining a safe distance away from both Michael and myself.

"So tell me, Phenex, what's the going rate now? Is it still thirty pieces of silver or did Michael offer you something better?" Phenex flinches but makes no move to defend himself, either physically or with those clever words that always seem to please him so.

And humanity has always been so convinced that pride is *my* sin.

I glance between the two of them. Michael spares only the shortest disdainful look at him, while Phenex sets his jaw, defiance flashing in his eyes, lit by the smallest ember of hope.

It dawns on me, and I let out a bark of laughter that he sold me out on a lie. "He offered you Heaven, didn't he?" Phenex nods, the movement barely perceptible, and I bite back the laughter that threatens to bubble out of me. "You're even more of a fool than I thought. Do you really think Michael would pollute Heaven with you?" The surety falters on Phenex's face and he looks to Michael, no doubt expecting my obedient brother to confirm their little deal, but Michael doesn't even deign to look at him.

"I'm not here for you, Lucifer." Michael rises from his seat, keeping his blade pointed to the floor and his arms wide, his stance wary but not aggressive. For the first time in our long lives, my brother doesn't look like he's itching for a fight.

That makes one of us then.

I strike quickly, aiming for an uppercut to his jaw that will send Michael flying through the wall, tearing through the skeleton of studs and burnt out electrical wires. I can already see him sprawled on the floor, those blue eyes dazed from the blow. I can feel his blood pouring over my hands, thick and sticky and *cleansing*.

I see it all so clearly that I almost don't register Michael blocking my punch with a meaty forearm. A sharp left hook strikes my cheek, snapping my head to the side. I shake off the ringing in my ears, rolling my shoulders as I prepare to dart forward and end this, but Michael's blade rests against my throat, shoving me against the wall.

A broken copper pipe digs into my back as Michael pins me, and the blood wells up against the shallow wound the blade carves into my neck.

His grip on the blade is slacker than it should be. Michael has never been one for gloating. Almost idly I wonder why I'm still alive.

"That was for yesterday."

The blade disappears from my throat, and Michael takes a few steps backward, thick muscles tense as he waits to see if I plan to attack again.

I consider it. This man with his military cropped hair and ill-fitting suit only vaguely resembles my holier-than-thou brother who always chose to follow the rules, even at the expense of his own happiness. *That* is the Michael I want to rip apart, not this hesitating creature unwilling to strike a killing blow.

I'm tired.

Tired of all of it. I left the only person that has made me feel alive in thousands of years broken and hating me. I want this to be done so I can return to Hell and bury myself in the screams of the damned until I *forget*.

"We may have had our disagreements, brother-" Michael begins, lowering his blade in a way that's supposed to what-placate me?

Anger surges through me, and I interrupt him. "-You sold me out all those years ago, Michael. That's a bit more than a disagreement."

Michael's next words are quiet, as he refuses to let himself be drawn back into the ancient feud. "Do you honestly think I'd let our Father's world burn?" When I remain silent, he continues. "Some of us grew out of our angry adolescence a long time ago, Lucifer. Some of us still do see it as our responsibility to protect our father's creations."

Michael's revelation sends me reeling. "If not you, then who is causing this? Only an Archangel would have the power."

"Uriel."

I scoff at the memory of the tall, lumbering angel more concerned with watching the flowers grow in Eden than picking a side during the war. "The guard dog of Eden? I must have hit you harder than I thought."

Michael soldiers on as if I haven't spoken. "He's gone quite mad, Lucifer. Solitude can do that."

"You don't say."

Michael has the courtesy to look shamed for a moment before the familiar earnest look returns to his face. "He wants to cleanse the world of the plague of humanity. Blight their souls with the Hellbound, sacrifice the girl to wash them clean, and scorch the world into a new Eden."

Every part of me goes cold at the word *sacrifice*.

"The girl has a name."

The dumbfounded look on Michael's face would be comical in any other circumstance. If only I'd know what it took to shut my brother up years ago.

Incredulous, he says, "You actually feel something for her, don't you?" When I don't instantly refute him, he shakes his head, wonder written on every inch of his face. "That certainly must have been a shock." Michael pushes past his surprise and is quickly all business again. "If you want her to live, stopping Uriel is her only chance."

Phenex shuffles his feet from the doorway, reminding us both of his presence. I glare at him, but agree reluctantly.

We split up to cover more ground – the word *sacrifice* still echoing in my mind.

❧ 16 ❧

GRACE

I sit for hours. The sunlight blazes through the plate glass window behind me, heating my skin, but I make no move to get up. Sweat trickles down my neck, the bright light scorching my back while the rest of me is so cold.

Faintly, I hear the noises of the hotel. The muffled thumps of footsteps and the low murmur of voices as the other guests file through the hallway. The metallic ding of the elevator. The quiet whoosh of the air conditioner kicking on.

The bright light of the afternoon gives way to sunset, painting the cream-colored walls with fiery streaks of crimson and gold before fading into purple and finally black.

The glass behind me cools as the stifling heat of day slips into the more moderate humidity of the evening.

I stare at the door, not wanting to admit to myself that all I want is for that smooth white door to open.

He isn't coming back. I was just a bit of shore leave. I swipe at the tears that prick in my eyes with the back of my hand, knowing that if I let myself cry, if I let myself be anything but numb, it's all over.

How long had he been laughing at me? The stupid human girl who let herself-

I pull myself upright, cutting that thought off before my brain can complete it, and rub the stiffness out of my legs. My body aches from sitting frozen for so long, and I welcome the physical pain. Anything to distract me from the whispers in my mind.

He was just using you.

Michael was right.

The person who murdered my family turned out to be the only honest one.

The strength that I'm only just starting to have a rein on twists inside me with the urge to lash out and destroy *something*, and I wonder how much of what I'm feeling is my own hurt boiling into anger and how much comes from Lucifer.

Even if I never see him again, I'll never be free of him.

I wander around the room, collecting my few possessions strewn around the suite. I grab a black ballet flat half-hidden under the couch and clamp down on the memory of Lucifer sliding the shoe off my foot and kissing my ankle before his hand drifted higher, the seductive smile on his lips so different than the cruel smirk it contorted into later.

Packing doesn't take nearly enough time. Once the bag is stuffed comes the realization that I have no place else to go. My home isn't safe, and I can't afford a hotel anywhere else.

The dull grey coin catches my eye where it rests, abandoned on the coffee table. I pick it up, running my fingers over the angular sigil etched into the smooth iron for the hundredth time before putting it back down. I stand up and walk out without looking back.

———

WANDERING the streets when you have a death warrant on

your head is about the worst thing you can do, so of course, that's exactly what I did. The crowds are thinner than normal, even for a weekday night, but what they lack in volume they make up for in vigor. A group of men passes me, dressed in the fratboy uniform of cargo shorts and popped collar polos. The one holding up the rear of the pack stops and turns to me, the smile on his lips not reaching his black eyes.

I take a step closer to him, loosening the tight leash on my new abilities, and he shrinks back with the recognition of a hyena meeting a much larger predator.

Thank you, Lucifer.

The thought comes to my mind unbidden, unwanted.

The men move on, no doubt searching for some easier prey, and I wonder what's wrong with me that I can't bring myself to care about her or the ugly fate rushing toward her.

I find myself in front of Spirits. The clock ticks over to 2 AM, and the open sign still glows neon green in the window, but the small bar is deserted except for Talia wiping down the counter.

I hesitate, my hand on the door. Is it even fair for me to draw her into the shitshow of my life?

Talia glances up and sees me. Her dark eyes widen as she takes in my disheveled appearance and the heavy suitcase slung over my shoulder. A moment later she's at the door, wrenching it open and pulling me inside. She clicks the lock behind me and slaps the button to turn off the open sign, all efficiency of movement, before turning to me with crossed arms and an arched eyebrow as she waits for me to explain myself.

I open my mouth to speak but freeze. I can't very well tell her I'm caught in the middle of an angelic pissing match between Heaven and Hell. I've seen concrete proof, and I still barely believe it.

"I didn't know where else to go," I murmur, my voice thick as I try to shove my thawed heart back into the deep freeze.

"You look like Hell," Talia says simply. "That's about the only reason I'm not laying into you for disappearing for a damn week without telling anyone." Talia ducks behind the counter and grabs a clean rag, thrusting it and the spray bottle of cheap cleaner into my hands. "The sooner you help me close up, the sooner we can get out of here and talk."

I drop my bag unceremoniously by the door and crouch down in front of the counter, mechanically wiping down the sticky mess of dried Hurricanes splattered across the front, thankful Talia has given me a reprieve, at least for a few minutes.

I watch her out of the corner of my eye, a whirlwind of movement as she scrubs down the countertops, counts the cash in the register, and restocks the racks of plastic cups. Talia's one of those people who always seems to have it together.

I bet she wouldn't fall in love with the Devil.

My hand falls to my side, the sharp scent of bleach filling my nose as the cleaner drips over my fingers.

If Talia speaks, I don't hear it. The roaring of my own heartbeat through my ears blocks it out. I sit down, my mind passively registering that Talia must have already mopped because the floor in front of the counter is usually sticky. More than a few tourists have lost a flip-flop that ends up stapled above our wall of shame in the back.

I gulp down mouthfuls of air, trying to bring the world back into focus.

"He really did a number on you, whoever he was."

I open my eyes to see Talia crouched beside me, her hand gently smoothing back a tangled curl from my forehead. I didn't even realize I had closed my eyes.

I get to my feet, shrugging off Talia's offered hand. She grins at that. "Good. You're still in there somewhere." Talia glances around the bar before nodding. "Clean enough. God knows it's cleaner than it ever is when Jimmy closes." Her face sobers as she catches sight of my suitcase by the door.

"Come on, let's go home."

TALIA LIVES in a small shotgun house a few miles from my neighborhood. Two large potted geraniums stand on either side of the door, the flame red flowers brightening the faded green of the paint. A few June bugs dart around the porch light, their bodies making tiny plinking sounds as they launch themselves at the bulb.

Talia unlocks the two deadbolts before creeping inside, flicking the porch light off behind her and plunging the doorway into darkness. She walks into the house without turning on a light, moving with the surety of someone who knows there's nothing waiting in the darkness.

I pull the door shut behind me, stepping over the threshold and fastening the locks before following Talia into the kitchen. She disappears down the hallway, ducking into one of the bedrooms and I hear the low murmur of her voice as she speaks to her husband.

I've never met Andre, only knowing that they'd been high school sweethearts. Andre works at an office job he hates during the day, filling in endless meaningless spreadsheets for a mid-market import company and taking afternoon and evening classes working toward a nursing degree.

Their daughter Sasha is five, a cheerful girl with a wide grin and her mother's serious eyes. She stares up from Talia's phone whenever a notification pops up, the background photo achingly familiar.

The same photo is stuck to the fridge, a pink plastic magnet in the shape of an S holding it up. In the photo, Andre and Talia gaze at each other instead of the camera. One of her braids curls around his finger, and they both have soft, adoring smiles across their lips, smiles only for each other, the camera forgotten. Between them, Sasha stares up at the camera, those huge eyes secure with the rightness of her small world.

I run my fingertips over the smooth surface of the photo, my mind seeing a similar one tucked in the frame of my bedroom mirror. The edges of that photo are worn, the sharp points rounded over the years, and the color has faded, sunlight lightening the deep tones into washed out golds and rusty coppers.

We were in the park. My Mom's hair was tied in a messy braid, but a few errant curls still escaped. A handful of white daisies plucked from the ground were tucked in the twists of the braid. A wide smile pulled her lips back and bared her teeth as she laughed at my Dad, a clumsily made daisy chain draped on his head like a jaunty crown. Between the two of them, I studiously braided together more flowers, completely ignoring the camera with my laser focus on my project.

I can't bring her into this.

I back away from the photo, reaching for my bag and turning quietly, intending to duck out the front door and away from Talia's idyllic life before I can destroy it.

My meeting with Michael taught me one valuable lesson. The Celestin women are poison. We destroy everything we touch, and Talia doesn't deserve to end up as collateral damage.

I'm halfway to the door when Talia's voice rings out.

"Going somewhere?"

I stop but don't turn around. "This was a mistake. I shouldn't have involved you in this."

I look back. Talia stands in the doorway, her face cast in shadow as the bright kitchen lights silhouette her. I don't need to see her face to know the look she's wearing.

Talia crosses the small room in a few strides and takes the suitcase from my slack fingers, tucking it next to the inviting looking sofa before leading me back into the kitchen.

"Sit." Obediently, I do. Talia may not be the official boss of Spirits but everyone looks to her, and everyone in the bar has been on the wrong end of her "Mama voice" at least once.

"I don't know you that well, Grace," Talia says, grabbing an unlabeled bottle filled with a clear, yellowish liquid from the top of the refrigerator. She plunks the bottle onto the table, grabbing a pitcher of cold water from the fridge and two heavy glass tumblers. "I don't really think anyone knows you," she continues, pouring a generous amount of the yellow liquid into each glass. "I'd say that I think you like it that way, but I don't think you do." She fills the remainder of the glass with the cold water, swirling the mixture until it turns a milky, pale yellow before handing me a glass.

I take a sip and the sharp, herbal flavor of licorice fills my mouth. "Homemade pastis. My grandma's recipe." She takes a long sip of her own drink before sitting down in the chair opposite me. "I thought about making tea, but it's too damn hot and this seems like a conversation for something stronger. So what's his name?"

I swallow, staring into the cloudy depths of my drink. "Lu-Luke," I answer. If Talia hears the lie, she doesn't comment.

"I saw you a week ago, and you were yourself. Or at least you seemed to be." Talia reaches across the table and covers my hand with hers, her skin warm and just a bit dry from the awful cleaners they make us use at work. She squeezes my hand, and for the first time since this all started, I feel like I'm back in the real world. "How did this Luke get you so turned around so fast?"

"Someone was. . . stalking me," I speak haltingly, picking each word carefully. Talia's demeanor instantly changes at those words, her back going rigid and her eyes hardening.

"Do I need to take you to file a police report, honey?" she asks, the softness in her voice a stark contrast to the anger on her face. "Did this guy hurt you?"

I shake my head wildly. "Not him. Lu-Luke knew the guy who was after me. It was his brother, and he put a stop to it. Or he tried to. Things got *intense* between us quickly." I take another sip of the pastis, my mind slipping back to our first kiss and the taste of heat and smoke and sin on his lips. *Intense* was right.

"His family. . . they're not good people. They're involved in some really messed up things. Luke's sort of the black sheep." I pause, calling up the memories of every creative writing class I've ever taken to spin Lucifer's fall from Heaven into a plausible story for 21st century New Orleans. "His Dad made him take the fall for something he didn't do, and he just got back."

"He was in prison, and his Daddy put him there?"

I nod, thankful that Talia seems to be buying my explanation. "Apparently his family was involved with mine back in the day. Some age-old vendetta that I had no idea about, but I still ended up getting dragged into."

I see Talia's mind racing a mile a minute as she pieces together my story with the scant details she knows about my past. A sharp intake of breath signals that she's reached the conclusion I'm leading her to. "You said your parents were killed when you were in high school. Did-" her question dies as she sees the look on my face. "His family had something to do with it."

"That same older brother."

"Shit." Talia sits back, the wooden chair creaking with her

movement as she struggles to think of what to say. "I'm sorry."

"It was a long time ago, but that's why it was a mistake for me to come here. I can't risk that they come looking for me. You have a family."

"Do you seriously think I'm going to let you leave after hearing that?" I open my mouth to protest. "No buts, girl. You're here now, and no one but me and Andre knows where you are. You're safer here than you'd be anywhere else." She presses her lips together, as she searches for her next words. "But why are you here instead of with your new man?"

"He's not my new anything," I say dully. "He made that clear."

"Are you sure?"

"Very." I drain the last watery dregs from my glass. "The things he said to me before he left." I stare down at my hands resting on the worn wood table, trying not to remember. "He said I was just a bit of entertainment. A distraction. Fucking shore leave." I can't keep the bitterness out of my voice as I study the tabletop, not wanting to see the pity in Talia's eyes.

"You said his family's dangerous. Did you think for a moment he might be afraid of what they'd do to you if they figured out you meant something to him?"

I snap my head up, staring at Talia with disbelief. I want to believe it, but Lucifer has never stuck me as someone who does anything he doesn't want to do. I shake my head. "You didn't see him. It wasn't just what he said. Everything about him was different. It's the only time I've ever been afraid of him."

"I wouldn't write him off just yet."

My eyelids feel heavy, the emotional upheaval of the day finally exhausting the last reserves of strength in me. Combined with the alcohol and the soothing warmth of Talia's kitchen, I'm fading fast.

"You're dead on your feet." Talia says, standing up quickly and ducking into the darkness of the hallway again. A moment later she reappears with a blanket and pillow in her arms, the pale blue fabric folded neatly and smelling faintly of lavender. "Get some rest. The couch is old but it's comfortable. I'll try to keep Sasha out of your hair when she wakes up, but no promises."

I nod gratefully, taking the blanket and pillow and moving into the darkened living room, leaving Talia to fall back into her normal routine. I sink down into the soft cushions, kicking off my shoes as an afterthought. I'm dimly aware of the faucet running as Talia rinses out the glasses, but then she flips off the light and plunges the room into darkness.

I pull the blanket over my body, the familiar smell of lavender oil increasing with the blanket unfolded. As I drift off, the bond between us pulses faintly, and in that hazy state between sleep and wakefulness, it comforts me.

I sleep without dreams.

"ARE you my Mama's new friend?"

The small voice a few inches from my face jolts me awake. Perched on the edge of the coffee table is Sasha, watching me warily. I sit up slowly, squinting at the clock on the wall ticking cheerfully. Nine thirty.

"I am," I reply, "My name's Grace." Sasha beams, and I find myself returning her infectious smile. The savory smell of bacon frying wafts to me, and I hear the sound of plates clattering in the kitchen.

"You up, Grace?" Talia calls. "I tried to keep her from waking you up as long as I could, but we don't get too many guests, so you're pretty fascinating."

I let Sasha lead me into the kitchen, shaking the last

vestiges of sleep from my brain. Talia looks more awake and aware than anyone running on less than six hours of sleep has the right to. "Bathroom's down the hall. Food should be ready in about ten minutes or so."

The sounds of Sasha chattering away to Talia as she cooks follows me down the hallway, a buzz of childish exuberance over the backdrop of Talia humming. I pull the bathroom door shut behind me, muffling their voices as I splash water on my face and try to wrangle my hair into something resembling presentable.

I twist my hair into a simple braid, trying to avoid looking into the mirror as much as possible, but I still see the dark shadows circling my eyes and the brittle smile across my lips. Even after a night's sleep I feel strung out, my body needing his presence.

Is this what I'm doomed to for the rest of my life? Craving Lucifer like an addict when he doesn't even want me?

"Grace! Food's ready!"

Forcing my smile a bit wider, I open the door and join them.

"YOU DON'T HAVE to pretend for me."

The food is hearty and simple. Sasha talks a mile a minute, peppering me with the essential details of her young life like how her kindergarten class has a bunny named Pecan and how she wants to be an animal doctor when she grows up, "Just like Daddy's going to be, but with puppies!" Talia smiles at that, pride beaming out of her like morning sunshine.

I studiously avoid focusing too much attention on either of them, not wanting to intrude on their minds when I'm already imposing on their lives.

Sasha disappears into the living room, sprawling out on her stomach with a coloring book and a Ziploc baggie filled with crayons next to her, humming tunelessly to herself as she fills in the picture of a butterfly with pink and purple and yellow.

Talia wanders through the house, a laundry basket balanced on her hip as she collects errant socks and t-shirts abandoned during the last few days of activity. "You're going through a lot, Grace," she continues, effortlessly picking up last night's conversation. "I know we're not exactly at the exchanging friendship bracelets stage yet, but you don't have to pretend everything is okay either."

A tenseness that I didn't realize was there drains out of my shoulders at her words. "I just don't know how to do this. I should hate him for what he said to me. Part of me does," I finish lamely, hearing the lie in my voice.

Talia glances over her shoulder at me as she drops the basket by the door for a trip to the Laundromat later. "Look, I'm just an impartial observer. I don't know him or his side of this, but it still sounds to me like everything he said to you was to get you away from him and out of his family's sights."

I want to believe it. I don't even know if he *can* be killed, but the way he talked about destroying Michael had to mean it was a possibility. And the thought of Michael turning his own weapon on Lucifer and stealing another person I love has my throat closing up.

There's that word again.

The realization that I love him isn't met with a choked panic attack on the floor of a dive bar this time, but it's no easier to handle in Talia's cheerful kitchen surrounded by reminders of the happy, normal life I'll never have, even if I do manage to survive this.

"Maybe he was right," I breathe, not wanting to speak the words aloud. Saying something out loud gives it power, after all. "Maybe I should stay away. Just go back to slinging shots at Spirits and forget about him and all this insanity that my life has turned into."

"You could." My head jerks up, staring at Talia and the smug smile she wears at my disbelief. "Thought so. That's not what you want."

"Yeah, well he didn't really consider what I wanted yesterday," I say sardonically. "He just ended it."

"So give him a few days to regret it, and then go find him and un-end it."

I open my mouth to tell Talia that it isn't that easy but fall silent.

Finally, after a long stretch of quiet, I add. "It's not that simple."

Talia dismisses that with a roll of her eyes. "If he means that much to you, you make it that simple."

❧ 17 ❧

LUCIFER

The city stretches out before me. From the roof of The Saint, the traffic-choked streets are nothing more than streaks of red and white light, racing toward their destination at an irritated crawl. Street lamps illuminate the insect-sized humans going about their night.

If more sirens screech through the night than usual as the local law enforcement futilely tries to subdue this sudden epidemic of unnaturally strong, rage-filled criminals prowling the streets, it certainly doesn't have much of an effect on the crowds. I'm not surprised. Nero and his fiddle might have been a myth but the brothels and taverns were still packed when Rome burned. Two thousand years and beyond trading the town crier for Twitter, nothing has changed.

And somewhere, down in the thick of all of it, is Grace.

Her presence tugs at me, a persistent throb in the depths of my brain reminding me that I can send her away but not truly banish her.

I take a long pull from the bottle of whiskey in my hand. I'd returned after a day of fruitless searching for Uriel. A few days ago, the advances of the bartender pouring my drink, his fingers lingering over mine just a bit longer than necessary as he handed me the glass, would have been a welcome diversion. The cocktail waitress who sidled up next to me with a white dress clinging to her generous curves could have rounded out the trio nicely.

Instead, I found myself gritting my teeth and ignoring them, the very desires I had reveled in grating on my nerves until I grabbed the bottle of whiskey in front of me and stalked away.

The door to the roof was shut tight, but a quick twist of the knob snapped the locking mechanism, and a flight of stairs later, here I am, a dozen stories above the city, caught between Heaven and the muck of the world.

Humanity isn't the only thing that doesn't change, it seems.

Tilting my head back to gaze at the cloudless night sky, the darkness broken by pinpricks of the stars I lit so many eons ago, I glower at the blackness.

"I bet you think this is hilarious. I come up here to clean up YOUR MESS, and this happens." I tip back the bottle, taking another swig and coming up empty, envying the weak mortal constitution for the first time. Getting blackout drunk unquestionably has an appeal, especially now.

"I bet you're up there enjoying your cosmic fucking gag reel at all of our expense," I spit, the bottle dangling limply from my fingers as I rail at the skies. "I could have killed Michael. Your precious, always obedient lap dog. You sit back and let Uriel slaughter his way through your own bloodline, and you do nothing!" I fling the bottle over the side, taking a tiny bit of satisfaction in the sudden blare of car horns as it shatters on the streets below.

"I don't know why I expected anything else from you. You have a habit of martyring your children to whatever cause you deem worthy, whether they consent or not."

The skies stay silent, the only movement from the blinking lights of a plane descending toward the airport.

"You did this. You put her in my path so that I could watch her die."

I hear the soft whoosh of displaced air behind me and turn to see Michael, his wings such a brilliant white they glow.

But not nearly as bright as mine once did.

If Michael heard my tirade, he chooses not to comment.

"Nothing. He's gone to ground," Michael says, looking irritated at the fruitless search that requires him to still be in my presence. "He'll let the city slip into chaos and wait for the girl to surface before he makes a move." Michael steps closer to me warily, vanishing his wings in the half-second between strides. "I know you have her stashed somewhere, Lucifer. Where is she?"

I exhale slowly, turning my back to Michael and returning my gaze out to the city.

"I don't know."

"I don't believe you."

"Believe whatever you want about me. That should be easy enough for you." I reach out across the bond just enough to let the faint pulse of her life reassure me before adding, "I won't make her a part of this. Dear old Dad has taken enough from her already."

I don't need to be facing Michael to see the righteous indignation across his face at my suggestion that our Father is responsible for the city's current predicament. "Our Father didn't order this Lucifer," Michael states with the assurance of a true believer. "Uriel chose to do this."

The zealots always were my favorites down in Hell.

I round on Michael, and something in my face makes him take a step back. "Choice." I mock. "The next thing you'll be saying is that he exercised his free will. Uriel always was a slow learner, wasn't he?" I take another step forward, but this time Michael holds his ground. We stand eye to eye under the unfeeling gaze of Heaven, and I'm just begging for an excuse to make my brother bleed.

Of course, there are so many ways to damage. I should know. I invented most of them.

"You and I though, we're different than Uriel. Neither of us ever doubted who we were." I tilt my head to the side, fixing Michael with an inquisitive look as I make the first cut. "Though you did have your little detour in Phoenicia all those years ago, didn't you?" Michael flinches but doesn't move, anger blazing in his eyes as I poke at the old wound.

Time to rip it open then.

"And how is dear Elissa? It's been some time since I spoke with her. I'm sure you've checked up on her over the years. Tell me, does she still despise you?"

I only have the tick of Michael's jaw as a warning, but I still easily dodge his punch.

"Temper temper. What would Dad say if he saw his sons fighting?"

"You're an ass."

"No, I'm just honest." I shift back on my heels, watching Michael warring internally with his urge to try for another punch and his strange desire to keep whatever tentative peace he can.

The momentary amusement of antagonizing my brother doesn't manage to lift my mood for long, and I pivot on my heel and walk back to the edge of the building, leaving Michael standing in the middle of the roof.

"Leave."

Filtered up a dozen stories, the noises of the city are muffled. Even the constant drone of mortal desire and sin that buzzes in my ears like an annoying insect is quieter. But the soft sound of the air displacing when Michael unfurls his wings and leaves me alone never comes.

"What do you think Uriel will do to her if he finds her first?" Michael's boots crunch on the loose gravel scattered across the tar as he walks to the edge, peering over the side to the city below. "You think I don't remember what it's like to be forced to choose between one of them and my duty?"

"Duty," I jeer, the word tasting foul in my mouth. "Do you think I give a damn about duty?" I fling my arm outward, gesturing at the masses below us. "I don't create evil. I punish it. You know that." In my peripheral vision, I see Michael cock his head in confusion, looking almost like he's seeing me for the first time. "I didn't come here to put a stop to this for Heaven. And honestly, it's not even for Hell. It's for them."

I lean on the railing, staring straight down at the grey pavement twelve floors below, the whispers of *LustGreedWrath* rising toward me like smoke. "I understand them. He created them and then set them adrift in this world. Our Father might be perfectly happy to wash his hands of his creations, but I'm not. Not anymore."

"You've changed, brother."

"A few thousand years gives you time to think." I glance over at Michael and see that his eyebrows have taken up permanent residence in his hairline, his utter shock over my apparently sudden change of heart written all over his countenance.

"It's probably best that you ended it now. You couldn't very well bring a living human with you back to Hell."

I bristle at Michael's assumption. The truth is until Grace innocently mentioned it the concept of staying never occurred to me. The plan started off so simple – sample the local flavor, kill my brother, restore the natural order, and return to Hell.

But Grace's words planted a seed. And Michael's statement that *of course*, I'm going back forces me to confront what she already knew.

I don't want to return to year upon year of blood and screams and misery. Hell can run without me. Let the Fallen and the demons have at it. I just want to be free.

"Who says I have any intention of going back?"

Michael sputters, "But you have to go back!" with such vehemence that it's almost comical. Pity I'm not in the jovial mood.

"I have to go back?" I demand. "Or what? I'll be *punished*? Please enlighten me as to what retribution Father will bring on me that's worse than Hell!"

Michael holds his tongue for longer than I expect before saying, "Hell needs a guardian."

"Are you volunteering? Because I think there's a permanent vacancy coming open." When Michael opens his mouth to argue again, I say one word, my voice low and dangerous as I reach the end of my patience.

"Leave."

Incredibly enough, he does. I hear the whisper of his flight feathers across the air as he leaves me alone with my thoughts, the edges of the sky just starting to lighten with the coming dawn.

INTERLUDE
PHENEX

MOST ANGELS, Fallen or otherwise, would resent a task as insultingly simplistic as staking out a human's house, but Phenex has never been one to follow the beaten path. The address Lucifer provided looks no different than every other house nearby, the goldenrod yellow door the only thing differentiating it from the other long, low shotgun houses on the street.

A large ginger cat naps on the front porch, its eyes opening to warily watch Phenex as he ascends the stairs to the door. It meows softly in greeting before closing its green eyes, unmistakably finding Phenex unworthy of attention.

The old lock gives way quickly under Phenex's hand, the pieces of the bolt rattling inside the door as Phenex enters, pulling it shut behind him.

When a quick sweep of the small house reveals that Phenex is its lone occupant, his natural curiosity quickly takes over. "What is it about this girl that has Lucifer so infatuated?" he murmurs.

The house is sparsely decorated, the walls bare beyond a few paintings hung haphazardly in the living room. The largest dominates the back wall, and from a few feet away the entire canvas appears to be painted black. As Phenex draws closer the early morning light filters in from the shuttered window and catches on streaks of charcoal grey and paler shades of smoke. The fallen angel scrutinizes the canvas, and the whorls of darkness finally coalesce into a massive set of jet black wings, drops of iridescence in the paint making them appear to glow from within.

Hidden in the bottom corner of the canvas, added as an afterthought below the tip of the right flight feather are the initials *MC*.

Phenex moves deeper into the house, wrinkling his nose at the wilted vase of white daisies next to the sink and the long crack in the glass cutting the window above in two. He crosses the threshold of the bedroom, idly noting the drawers gaping open, clothes spilling out onto the scarred wooden floors as though she had packed quickly.

Tucked into the large mirror above the dresser is a faded photo of a blonde woman nearly the image of Grace leaning against a red Jeep. She's laughing, her head thrown back with abandon, delight radiating off her. Phenex plucks the photo from its home, squinting at the worn paper, trying to reconcile that this wild, happy creature had born the girl he met.

Maybe that's what keeps drawing Lucifer to her. Hidden deep within both of them is the memory of joy before it was buried by the weight of their lives. And their choices. "It always comes back to free will," Phenex mutters, adding the pang at the loss of Lucifer's friendship to his endless litany of regrets.

Shaking his head at the sentimentality, Phenex exits the room, heading back to the living room and the lumpy looking couch by the window. If he's stuck waiting here for Uriel to show up, he hopes they at least have cable.

A soft scrape on the floor behind him is the only warning. Without bothering to look back, Phenex drops to a crouch, Uriel's blade whipping over his head close enough for the breeze to ruffle his pale hair.

Any triumph is short-lived. Uriel recovers from his miss quickly, backhanding Phenex with his free hand, the force knocking him into the coffee table. The glass top shatters under his weight.

Phenex rolls off the pile of rubble, narrowly escaping Uriel's blade as it slams down into the center of the table. He darts back, trying to keep some distance between himself and the larger angel.

The last time Phenex laid eyes upon Uriel was long before the Fall. Of the Archangels, only Lucifer bothered to interact with lower level seraphim like Phenex, the rest preferring to keep their own company, but the hazy memories Phenex has of Uriel guarding the gates of Eden with his flaming sword can't compare to the madness in his eyes now.

Uriel's bulky form is nearly as tall as Michael, with broad shoulders and a mane of dusty brown hair hanging to his shoulders, the ends rough as though he hacked them off with his blade. He probably had.

While most angels on Earth at least make a cursory attempt to match their clothing to the current century, Uriel dresses in the same style of rough-spun robes he wore in Heaven.

A quip about his fashion sense dies in Phenex's throat at the sight of Uriel's eyes. Far different than the haughty superiority of Michael or the tightly coiled wrath of Lucifer, Uriel's glimmer with the calm surety of a heretic staring down a blaze with a smile. Michael was right. He's completely insane.

There have been rumors sifting through Hell for years of an unknown angel, powerful and pitiless as any demon, who demands repentance before he cuts you down.

And if your repentance doesn't please him, the cuts are slow.

Phenex had laughed at the rumors. More often than not, demons are as bad as humans when it comes to making up frightening stories about the boogeyman in the closet.

Phenex isn't laughing now.

"This world was pure once," Uriel's voice is low and gravely from disuse. "I don't know what's worse, the stink of the humans and their petty lusts or the filth of the Fallen that choose to wallow with them." Uriel circles Phenex, cutting him off from escaping through the door or windows.

"If anyone could use some time in the thick of humanity, it's you," Phenex taunts. "Might yank that angelic stick out of your ass." Uriel lunges forward. Phenex leaps back, but not far enough. The blade slams into his side; the Heaven forged metal burning like acid.

Phenex's knees buckle, and Uriel wrenches the blade from him. He crashes gracelessly to the floor, coughing wetly as his body rejects the touch of the weapon.

Uriel kneels beside him, the rough brown fabric of his robes sopping up the blood already starting to pool beneath the smaller angel.

"I know who you are," Uriel says, his larger hand grabbing a fistful of Phenex's hair and hauling him up. "The pretty one who trails behind Lucifer like a pet, begging for his scraps while dreaming of Heaven." Uriel leans closer, and under the metallic tang of blood, Phenex can smell the warm earth of Eden still clinging to his skin. "We laugh at you."

Uriel releases him, and Phenex crumples to the ground, the vibrant red stain across his pale suit growing as he struggles to rise, preparing himself for Uriel's killing blow.

"You're not worth the effort," Uriel sneers, the sound of his boots fading as he walks out the door.

✿ 18 ✿

GRACE

"I don't want you going into work tonight."

Talia's head whips around in surprise to stare at Andre over the dining room table. "Did you hit the lotto on the way home from work and forget to tell me?" she teases.

Andre isn't smiling. I instantly liked Talia's husband. Quiet where she's outspoken, Andre strikes me as someone content to let his wife and daughter have the stage, and there haven't been any of the expected questions of how long until I'll be out of their hair. I have the feeling I'm not the first stray that Talia has brought home.

That quiet intensity makes both of us sit back and listen. "You never call out, and you said your boss barely notices who's there and who isn't anyway-"

"-You never had an issue with my job before," Talia interrupts.

Andre slaps his hand on the table. "Talia!" Instantly, he lowers his voice, looking guiltily down the darkened hallway to where he tucked Sasha into bed an hour ago. "Things are not okay out there right now." Andre shakes his head. "You know how we've been having practicals at the hospital the past few weeks? People have been coming in with these horrific injuries." Andre closes his eyes, wincing as he rubs the bridge of his nose. "I've seen things in the past week that no one should have to see. Horror movie shit. And I don't want you out there. Your job pays crap anyway. If you get fired, just move to another bar two doors down."

Talia opens her mouth to protest, but I speak up. "He's right."

Talia sighs, but sits back down into her chair, the matter effectively settled, at least for the moment. "It's not fair if it's two against one."

"Just turn on the TV or open up the news on your phone," I say. Pulling my phone out of my pocket, I scroll through the news feed, flipping past sports and weather before coming to local events. GRUESOME DOUBLE HOMICIDE the headline reads, the lurid photo of two bodies being wheeled out of a motel room splashed across the page below.

I skim the article until I reach the phrase *eyeballs appear to have been eaten*. Closing the tab quickly, I flip my phone over, leaving it face down in the middle of the table as I try to push that image out of my mind.

"And that's enough internet for today." I turn to Talia, seeing her eyes widen in shock at whatever she reads from her phone screen. Her finger keeps moving, scrolling through article after article with disbelief at the escalating poison that has infected the city.

Andre reaches across the table and takes the phone gently from her, setting it down before clasping her hand. "We can afford to have you miss a couple shifts. That bar's sketchy enough on a good day, but right now places like that are going to be a beacon for whatever the Hell is going on."

Talia nods in agreement, still looking shaken from whatever she read. Andre turns to me. "Same goes for you, Grace.

Since you're hiding out here anyway, I didn't really think you'd be planning on heading off to work."

"Not a chance," I reply.

"I'm not saying either of you have to stay locked in the house, but just be cautious. And stick together."

FOR ALL HER willingness to go along with our worry over what's happening in the city, Talia is still practical to a fault. And the needs of her family certainly outweigh a little concern about an uptick in crime.

After two days of skipping work and not leaving the house except for the short drives to Sasha's school, we're both going stir crazy, but it's the overflowing laundry basket that finally pushes Talia over the edge.

It's Saturday afternoon, and while Sasha colors on the living room floor, her pink sock-clad feet bouncing excitedly as she fills in the outline of a cow in fluorescent orange, Talia spends her energy glaring at the laundry basket.

"Can you watch Sasha for a couple hours? Andre's not going to have anything to wear to work Monday if I don't get this done. Especially with the extra weekend shifts."

Laundry day shouldn't fill me with apprehension, but every day that passes without an incident has me growing tenser. Like the last hours before a storm hits, the air feels charged. Something is coming, and I don't want Talia on the streets when it arrives.

Forcing a smile on my face, I turn to her. "Let me go." When Talia starts to protest, I interrupt. "The Laundromat's only a mile away. I'll have my phone the whole time, and I'll be back before you know it. I could use a little alone time to think." I pause before adding, "Maybe I'll give Luke a call. It's been a few days, so maybe I'll take your advice."

Talia grins, and I push down the guilt that rolls through me at manipulating her.

But I have to do this.

Just like in the bar, Talia runs a tight ship at home. Despite my repeated offers to help, there's never much to do. Everyone cleans up after themselves without any prodding, so I've been left with far too much time on my hands. The television is kept permanently tuned to the children's channels after Andre flipped to CNN and saw another grainy crime scene photo splashed across the screen as Sasha entered the room.

She'll learn about the ugliness in the world soon enough. Right now, we all want to shield her from what's happening outside the house.

Instead, I stay glued to my phone, watching as the body count ticks higher with each passing hour, hating myself for every innocent person that ends up infected with a Hellbound soul and for the havoc they move on to cause.

I have to stop it.

Lucifer believes that killing Michael will put a stop to it all and set everything to rights. I don't know if I'm still mortal enough that killing Michael is an impossible dream, but I have to try. Even if I fail, maybe Lucifer can succeed.

As I load the laundry basket in the back of Talia's car and drive away, I only have one thought.

I'm done running.

INTERLUDE
MICHAEL

TWO DAYS of searching for Uriel and still nothing.

Michael sighs in irritation after another day of coming up

empty-handed. He has searched every chapel, every cemetery, anything that even hints at consecrated ground and still come up empty.

Up ahead the sign for the New Orleans Botanical Garden waits patiently, the heady scent of flowers and warm earth emanating past the gates, a little slice of Eden in the city center.

The day is warm but not oppressively so. The gardens should be swarmed with people, tourists looking for a respite from the man-made revels, children running through the patches of wildflowers, couples searching for a quiet spot alone among the roses. Instead, the parking lot sits empty, the gardens quiet.

Of course, that emptiness may have something to do with the tall robed man standing by the gate clutching a blood-stained sword in his burly fist.

Michael approaches cautiously. He and Uriel have never been particularly close. Even in the early days long before the Fall, Uriel had preferred his own company to the camaraderie of the garrison, and after Lucifer's defection, he withdrew even further, rarely leaving Eden. At the time, it had seemed better to leave him to his own devices.

That was obviously a mistake.

Michael eyes the sword, the blood on the blade long since dried, the streaks of gore looking nearly black on the bright silver. "Brother, what have you done?"

"Merely dispatched a Fallen that polluted this world with his presence." He lifts the sword, admiring the blood-stained blade. "Lucifer's little lap dog. The creature actually thought he could best me." Uriel throws back his head and laughs, and Michael barely represses a shiver at the chilling sound.

Abruptly, Uriel's laugh cuts off. His expression turns expectant as he asks, "Have you come to aid me in this fight, brother?" The look he wears is as welcoming as Uriel's face is capable of producing, but the expression quickly fades at Michael's silence. Almost imperceptibly his hand tightens around the hilt of his weapon.

Michael notices.

"So it's true then." His face turns stony, his lip curling in disgust. "I didn't want to believe what was said of you in the garrison, Michael. That you sympathize with these humans!"

"They are our Father's creations!" Michael explodes. "We are their shepherds, not their executioners. What you're doing to them is worse than any demon or Fallen."

"I am bringing them into paradise!" Uriel's shout echoes through the gardens, and even nature falls silent at his fury.

Michael keeps his voice even as he proceeds, knowing his brother's fuse grows shorter and shorter. "And what of the Last? She's far more than just another human. Her blood is divine. Harming her is not your place, Uriel."

Uriel spits on the ground. "She is an abomination. I meant to end her line years ago when I took her mother, but it was a fortuitous error. Her sacrifice will wash this world clean and bring forth another Eden."

Michael bows his head slightly, knowing there is no reasoning with his brother and raises his weapon.

Uriel already has his at the ready, the bloody edge glinting dully in the sun. "You remember what we used to do to traitors, don't you, brother?"

Michael has never been one for witty banter during fights. One didn't end up with the title of "God's most fearsome warrior" by focusing on anything but the most efficient way to kill.

Michael knows what name his brothers refer to him as behind his back. God's Poison. The one always willing to carry out any violent deeds his Creator demanded.

And demand He did.

Uriel wildly telegraphs his first strike as he swings his

blade with all the finesse of a human swinging a hatchet. Michael brings his own blade up to parry the stroke, the bones in his shoulder ringing with impact as he forces Uriel back through the garden gate.

Inside the walled garden is an explosion of color, swaths of wildflowers mingling with the more manicured plants. The tall brick of the walls blocks any breeze, leaving the air thick with the honey-sweet scent of pollen from a hundred different flowers.

Michael darts forward, aiming for a slash across Uriel's chest that never connects. With a surprising speed for his size, he dodges, and Michael ends up decapitating a few lilies, their bright orange petals scattering at his feet.

"It doesn't have to be this way, brother," Michael says, gritting his teeth as the next stroke makes contact, tearing a deep gash in Uriel's forearm. He doesn't even glance at the wound as the blood pours down. "We've had enough wars in Heaven. If you start another, you're no better than Lucifer was."

That's the wrong thing to say. With a snarl of incoherent rage, Uriel raises the sword above his head, bearing it down with a force meant to split Michael's skull in two. Michael thrusts his sword upward to block, but the angle is all wrong. Uriel's weapon glances off Michael's enough to save him from instantaneous death, but the sharp edge tears into his shoulder.

Michael's blade slips from nerveless fingers, and Uriel rocks back on his heels, his own weapon falling to his side as he gloats. "God's Poison seems weaker than he used to be. All this time away from Heaven. . . it reduces you. Makes you more like *them*. But we all remember your little sabbatical in Phoenicia with your blasphemous little whore. Even a thousand years later her stink is still on you."

Michael roars as he launches himself at Uriel, the

uppercut snapping the angel's jaw to the sky as his sword falls to the dirt. "This isn't about *me*, Uriel," Michael growls. Lucifer's mention of Elissa had reopened the wound he thought long healed, but that was expected. Lucifer has always been a champion of finding any weakness he can exploit, but what Uriel lacks in subtlety he makes up for in brute force.

And it's working. His battering ram approach will leave the city in ruins, but when winning is the only goal, the cost doesn't matter.

Uriel grabs Michael's injured shoulder, digging his fingers into the wound, tearing at the nerves and muscle until he touches bone. Michael snaps his head forward, colliding with Uriel's skull with enough force to daze them both.

His grip loosens enough that Michael can wrench free, swiping his sword from the ground and backing toward the gate.

"Planning to run, brother?" Uriel taunts. "I never thought I'd see the day when Michael backed down from a fight. How things have changed since our younger days."

Hot shame floods Michael. Uriel is right, after all. He's the one who never backs down from a fight, who always obeys. Only once has he refused an order, and he has long since paid for that transgression.

But destroying another Archangel. . . for all of Uriel's sins, he has not Fallen. His death has not been ordered by their Father. Michael knows he's been fighting to wound, not to kill. Uriel has no such qualms.

Spreading his wings, Michael flies.

Heaven or Hell-forged weapons are all that can injure or kill an angel. The wound was not lethal, and Michael can already feel the muscle and sinew slowly knitting back together. He lands on a roof, some anonymous office building, all cheap tar and scattered trash from employees that use the barren spot as an escape.

Michael's knees buckle when he lands, and he throws out his undamaged arm, barely catching himself from getting a face full of gravel. Michael rolls over, his wings cushioning his back as he stares up at the unflinching brightness of the sky, and for the second time in his long existence Michael feels doubt.

THE LAUNDROMAT IS DESERTED.

On a Saturday afternoon, it should be choked with people, every washer whirring and spinning as they fill the air with the chemical scents of detergent — acrid approximations of "clean rain" and "floral meadow." It should be hot, the air conditioning fighting a losing battle with the heat from a dozen bodies and the humidity from the poorly sealed dryers.

Instead, the metallic ding of the sliding door echoes off the industrial beige walls. The molded plastic chairs sit empty. A few forgotten articles of clothing rest discarded on one of the scarred folding tables — mismatched socks, their mates lost in the black hole of the dryer, a bleach stained t-shirt, a frayed bandana. Even the old tube TV bolted to the corner of the room is silent.

Chiding myself at being unnerved by a Laundromat of all things, I quickly load the machines, separating out colors and whites by muscle memory as my mind wanders.

I feel the same prickling on the back of my neck telling me that however empty the building might look, someone is watching.

The metallic creaks of the overworked engines of the washers sound loud in the vacant room. I sit down on one of the chairs, the hard plastic digging into my spine as I wait, tamping down the nervous energy that makes me want to do anything but sit still.

I meant it when I said I wanted time to think, though contacting Lucifer isn't nearly as simple as making a phone call.

The sensation of being watched increases to an almost physical heaviness pressing down on my chest. A low rumble, more vibration than audible sound, fills the room. Shards of glass fly from the tv screen as the cathode tube ruptures, the pressure releasing a loud boom. I jump up from the chair, turning to face the bank of windows that makes up the front wall.

"Lucifer?" I call, the false bravado in my voice comforting me more than it should considering that no part of me actually expects it to be him. I watch as long cracks split the glass panes, the pressure growing until even breathing hurts.

Like a sonic boom from a jet, the release of pressure hits with a thunderclap. The fissures in the glass collapse in on themselves as the windows crumble, pebbles of safety glass raining down into the street. The sounds of dozens of car alarms blare, the klaxon of different horns deafening.

I push open the door, the half-destroyed doorbell dinging on my exit like a dying animal as I walk out into the street.

No one.

I expect Michael to be waiting, but the streets are empty. I glance at Talia's car, wincing at the spiderweb cracks across her windshield, before walking past it.

Michael found me. There's no way I'm risking leading him back to Talia's house.

I'm sorry, I say silently, knowing that if I disappear Talia will blame herself for letting me go.

I walk. Barren of people, the streets are quieter than I've ever seen them. Even in the aftermath of the worst hurricanes, the sounds of sirens and voices had still been present. Never this oppressive silence.

I turn onto the next street, my feet unconsciously taking me back toward the city center, toward Bourbon, toward The Saint.

Toward where it all started.

As I turn down Treme Street, I see the crowd, and for the barest instant, I relax before I notice the way they move. This isn't the usual group milling outside a trendy restaurant or ogling a street performer. Their movements are all wrong, slow and jerky at once, as though the simple motion of walking has become foreign to them.

Almost like they aren't used to their own bodies.

With every step I take toward them the feeling of wrongness grows stronger, choking me like the scent of garbage rotting in the sun. The human part of me recoils in fear, but the divine part of me only pities them. But pity isn't going to stop the boldest of them from trying something.

The hope that they'll let me pass is short lived. The first woman that I cross paths with looks like someone's grandma, white curls fluffed out around a face twisted in an unnatural grimace. I pass granny and see a tall man wearing a fast food uniform, the garish yellow fabric stained with what I hope is ketchup.

It probably isn't ketchup.

I move around him slowly, watching from the corner of my eye as he cranes his neck to keep staring, his black eyes focused on me.

They fill in the gap I leave behind me, closing their ranks around and trapping me in. A meaty arm darts out and grabs me, thick fingers closing around my arm and jerking me deeper into the crowd.

The tourist who has my arm wears a neon green sweatshirt with *Welcome to New Orleans* scrawled across the front and a few strands of purple plastic beads hang around his neck. The only thing missing is the fanny pack. His beady black eyes glint in hunger as he pulls me closer to his face, choking me with his hot, fetid breath.

Not like this.

I flail wildly with my free arm, feeling the power surge up in me, fueled by the anger at what these creatures are doing to my city and the fear for everyone I care for. I've never thrown a punch in my life, but when my fist connects with the side of his head, the tourist staggers back and releases my arm.

With both hands free, I spread my arms wide, calling up everything I can think of – chanting the name of everyone that matters in my head like a mantra.

Mom.

Dad.

Talia.

Lucifer.

Lucifer.

Another set of hands reaches for my shoulder, trying to pull me off balance and drag me to the ground, but this time when the hands brush my skin, they instantly flinch back like I've burned them. Another woman dressed in a postal uniform grabs me only to let out a pained wheeze as her fingers grow red and raw at the brief touch.

I step forward, spreading my fingers wide and pressing my palms flat against the cheeks of the man in front of me. Once upon a time, he'd been good-looking, but now half his face is a ruin of bruises and lacerated skin. When my skin touches him, he shrieks, the sound barely human. The flesh blisters and peels under my fingertips, but still, I press harder, searing the outline of my hands into his tissue before snatching my hands back.

This time, they give me a wide berth, the soul-infected

humans staggering away from my poisonous touch. I move through them, and they part like water, closing their ranks behind me. The crowd grows thicker, and if not for their sudden fear causing them to give me space, I wouldn't be able to move.

I hear a scream, and through a break in the crowd, I see a woman being dragged into an alley. Further, in the distance, gunshots ring out, and the scent of burning gasoline hangs in the air from a car engulfed in flames in the middle of the road.

"Beautiful, isn't it?"

I freeze, turning around in a circle as I search for the origin of the voice, the crush of bodies disorienting me.

He slipped through the crowd unnoticed, the possessed souls avoiding his touch the way they avoid mine. *An angel,* my mind supplies unhelpfully. The fact that it isn't Michael standing before me offers little comfort. Dressed in worn robes that wouldn't look out of place on a medieval peasant, he doesn't exactly have the air of someone eager to make conversation.

But something about him is familiar. Rooted to the spot, we stare at each other, as I search the banks of my memory for the same square jaw and hate-filled eyes.

I've read stories where the main character receives a startling revelation and "felt the blood drain from their face," but the phrase always reminded me of one of those literary affectations that never actually happens to anyone.

Until today, at least.

My blood turns to ice, the cold sensation radiating outward into my limbs. I don't need to see my reflection to know that my skin has gone pale. My eyelids twitch in protest at being held open for so long. A quote from a half-remembered tv episode I watched in college repeats in my mind like a skipping record.

Don't blink.

And. . . he smiles. The expression looks wrong on his face, his lips stretched too wide, teeth bared too much, as though he's never seen a genuine smile and is working off a poorly written description. When he speaks again, his voice is a low rasp, rough and gravelly from disuse.

"You remember me then." It isn't a question.

Tom Petty was playing on the radio that day. "Free Fallin'" blared through the speakers while my parents sang along, loudly and more than a little off-key. My Dad slowed to a stop at a traffic light, drumming along with the song on the steering wheel before looking over his shoulder to flash me a grin.

"Come on, Gracie, next verse is yours!"

The light changed, and he started driving, humming along with the guitar solo. My Mom turned to ask me something, and she didn't see the tall man with wings appear in the middle of the road.

"DAD!" I screamed.

He cut the wheel hard to the right, and I felt the car tilt.

Then blackness.

Minutes or hours passed before I peeled my eyelids open, the smell of metal and gasoline thick around me. My head throbbed, and I touched my fingers tentatively to my temple. They came away sticky with congealing blood.

The Jeep had landed on the driver's side after it rolled. The radio had cut off but the turn signal still clicked, the metallic noise like a heartbeat as my fingers fumbled at the seatbelt.

I leaned forward as much as the belt would allow me. "Mom?" I whispered, my voice sounding smaller than it ever had. "Daddy?"

My father's neck was wrenched back at a terrifying angle, his eyes open and staring unseeingly out the shattered windshield. A low groan came from the passenger side, and my attention snapped to my mother. A thick shard of glass jammed into the juncture where her neck met her shoulder, the blood making her light hair look black. Her fingers pressed against the wound, trying to staunch the flood, but it continued to ooze through her fingers.

She coughed, the noise wet, and I thought of broken ribs and punctured lungs. When she spoke, blood stained her lips.

"I'm so sorry," she croaked, her free hand reaching between the bucket seats to grab my shirt, pulling me closer to her with a surprising amount of strength. "I tried. . . I tried to protect us from this. I'm so sorry, Gracie."

I heard the sound of sirens in the distance. I wanted to beg her to hold on, but my voice didn't work.

"Run. Run as far from this place as you can, and don't ever come back."

My mother's face blurred as the sirens grew louder. The sharp scent of ozone cut through the smell of blood and burning gasoline. As I slipped back into unconsciousness, I felt the car shift and heard the sound of metal tearing like paper, and my mother's voice, stronger than a dying woman's should have been, yelling, "You won't take her too!"

"IT WAS YOU."

The angel dips his head toward me, the barely perceptible nod infuriating me more than an evil cackle would have.

"You took everything away from me."

The off-kilter smile returns, and the angel takes another step closer, shoving aside a possessed human that blocks his path. "I did. It seemed only fair that your kind understand loss."

I stand my ground, drawing myself up to my full height that doesn't even reach the angel's shoulders. "You did this to the world." I look out at the mob at the angel's back, watching us impassively with those empty black eyes. "For what? Because you're angry that your Dad brought home a new baby and you're not the favorite anymore? And you say humans are the ones that are fucked up?"

Somewhere, Lucifer is chuckling at my words.

"You've been spending too much time with the Light-bringer, human," the angel snarls. "You forget yourself around your betters."

"And you forget that I'm not entirely human, angel," I reply.

Playing chicken with a psychotic angel isn't the smartest decision I've ever made, but finally seeing the face of my parent's killer has burned away the last vestiges of concern for my own safety.

You won't take her too!

My mother's last scream reverberates through my mind, the memory of the blinding light seeping in through my closed eyelids all those years ago filling me. "You tried to kill me that night, didn't you?" I ask. "And you failed. She stopped you."

If the angel has any concern about a repeat performance, he doesn't show it. "You're not the white witch your mother was. What do you have? Powers you don't understand how to harness and the stink of the Fallen on your skin. It's no matter though. I don't need you pure for my purposes." The angel draws a blade from the recesses of his robes, the same long, slender weapon I've seen in the hands of Lucifer and Michael.

And this one points right at me.

He took my father. My mother. The happy, normal life I was supposed to have.

He doesn't get to take me.

Not now.

Not today.

The power comes out of me like a punch, the same warm, white glow that made the tainted souls cower from me. The angel doesn't scare so easily though. Clenching my fists, I pull every shard of pain and loss that I've buried over the years, the emotions I swept aside like broken glass for my own survival. I compress it down into a ball of agony, dense as a dying star and dark as my father's lifeless eyes.

"I won't be needing this anymore," I say, locking my eyes with the angel's, re-building the connection between us that he forged with shattered glass and twisted metal seven years ago. "It's yours now."

I push.

A guttural scream rips free from the angel's throat as it strikes him, seven years of pain tearing through the neurons and synapses like a psychic bullet and driving him to his knees.

I'm not cocky enough to think I've won or done anything more than buy myself time. The crowd scatters, the possessed fleeing the divine power to search for more careless prey. I weave my way through the few that linger, moving as fast as I dare, praying to anyone who might still be listening that what I just did will leave the angel out of commission long enough for me to put some distance between us.

Don't run. It just gives them a reason to chase you.

The Saint looms up ahead, and I duck inside, slipping down the hallway. An abandoned room service tray sits by a door. I pick up the heavy black cloth napkin and wrap it around my elbow before jamming it against the fire alarm. The glass splits and I pull down the lever. An instant later, sirens blare through the hotel and doors start opening, travelers streaming out of the rooms, their faces a mixture of irritation and mild concern.

I ease past a slender redhead dragging a toddler behind her with less attention than she gives to her suitcase. In the back corner hides the service exit, the industrial red glow of the exit sign looking horribly out of place with the rest of the décor. Gratefully, I push the door open, the buzz from the alarm drowned out by the fire alarm.

I haven't even crossed the threshold of the door when I hear it.

"Grace."

I stop, standing in the doorway without looking back. Every cell in my body tunes to his presence.

Lucifer.

I knew he was here. I *felt* him the moment I entered the hotel, and if I had that awareness, there was no doubt in me that he'd known the instant I walked in.

I want to cling to my anger, to curse him for everything he put me through in the last few days. I want to tell him to leave, but I'm not stupid. The angel I just escaped from is still out there, and whether Michael is an enemy or just a bystander in this so is he. I need Lucifer. He used me, so I shouldn't have any qualms about using him to keep myself alive.

It all makes perfect sense until I turn and look at him.

He looks wrecked.

The immaculate black suit is no different, though his clothes seem like a cat obsessively cleaning itself, more of an ingrained habit than a real statement.

But everything else. . .

Lucifer scrubs his hand over the rasp of stubble on his face before letting it fall to his side. He keeps his eyes down-turned, carefully avoiding meeting mine. Then I blink and the mask is up, and he turns back into the same cold monster he'd been in the suite.

But now I know. I can't unsee what I just witnessed, but I can certainly play along for now.

Forcing myself into cool detachment, I ask. "So, what's the plan?"

✿ 19 ✿

LUCIFER

All I see is her.

Alarms blast around us, dozens of human voices adding to the din. Somewhere outside, Uriel's madness still ravages the streets.

But I forget it all at the sight of her trying to escape through a back door.

I felt her presence long before I saw her, the low-grade awareness in the back of my mind spiking with fear that had to mean Uriel had her within his sights. I'd been rushing toward the street, desperate to reach her before-

Then the rush of power detonating drove me to my knees. The missile wasn't aimed at me, so I only heard the echo of the screams, but it stopped Uriel, if only for a moment.

And whether it was instinct, muscle memory, or a side effect of that damned bond, she ran here. To me.

My hands twitch with the urge to pull her to me and never ever let her out of my sight again. And I've never been particularly good at ignoring my desires.

But it only takes a split second for it all to come crashing back. The prophecy. Her sacrifice. The entire reason I sent

her away in the first place. I shutter myself against her, ignoring the pang I feel as her face falls at my actions. It only takes a moment for Grace to school her features into an approximation of my own coldness.

Good. She's learning.

She might live through this yet, and then maybe-

I cut that thought off before it can take root. If the past week has given me anything at all, it's taught me that hope isn't made for someone like me.

"I'm guessing you met Uriel." The fire alarm cuts off, the sudden silence jarring. I glance around quickly. The hotel has emptied out, and while the crowds milling around in front of the building block the view of the street, we're still far too exposed for my liking.

I brush my hand over Grace's shoulder to steer her through the service door, barely hiding the tremor in my fingers when I touch her bare skin.

"Uriel," she says, artificial levity filling her voice. "Batshit crazy and dresses like the kid who got picked last at the renaissance faire?"

I can't help snickering at her description. "Very apt," I agree before sobering. "It's him that we're after, not Michael. Shockingly enough, Michael and I seem to be on the same side." The door shuts behind us, dumping us out in an alley behind The Saint, the corridor empty except for a few recycling bins overflowing with cardboard boxes.

Grace trails close behind me down the alleyway and for the next few blocks but balks when we reach the steps of the church, digging her proverbial heels into the pavement.

"Won't it be even easier for him to find us here?"

She's right, but if I can stash her somewhere safe, I can double back and *end this*. Impatient, I snap, "Perhaps, but I don't see a lot of other options. That crowd and your little display will only distract Uriel for so long."

With the immediate threat of death a few streets away, Grace's anger flares and she turns the ire on me full blast. "Why does it even matter to you what happens to me? I'm surprised you aren't offering to trade me to Uriel!"

I clench my jaw hard enough that my teeth ache to keep from grabbing her and shaking her. "Maybe I care because your inability to listen to reason and keep yourself hidden is forcing me to constantly rescue you."

Grace pushes past me, deliberately shaking off the hand that still rests on her shoulder. She pauses in the doorway, her face unreadable. "Don't do me any favors. You're the Devil, after all. I wouldn't want you to go against your nature." She turns her back on me and strides into the church without waiting to see if I follow, leaving the door gaping behind her.

Stung, I walk into the church, slamming the door shut behind us.

The small church sits empty, the parishioners having abandoned the simple building for the more ostentatious structures uptown. Fire and brimstone always seems much more palatable with a few golden candlesticks and a nice stained glass window to look at. A thick layer of dust covers the plain wooden pews, and the faint scents of incense and candle wax cling to the stones, the silence heavy in the stale air.

Grace stands before the altar – the plain dais as unadorned as everything else in the church. Countless hands have smoothed the raw wood and stone to a satin finish, adding the simple cross carved into the center as the only adornment.

Her head remains bowed when she speaks again. "I never asked for any of this. I didn't want to be special. I didn't want to know that an angel murdered my parents because of some vendetta against humanity that we had nothing to do with. You should have left me in that bar."

She lays her hand on the altar, her fingers tracing the cross. "I should feel something from this, shouldn't I? We're in a church. If my blood is so holy why are you the only thing that makes me feel *anything*?"

I walk the length of the aisle without realizing it, moving as close to her as I dare. I stop at the bottom of the three short steps leading up to the raised platform that holds the altar, knowing that if I take those last steps I'll never let her go. She turns, and the look on her face is so stricken, so utterly *familiar* that I mount the stairs and pull her to me in a single heartbeat.

Grace melts against me, and for the first time in days, the bond isn't at the forefront of my mind. A breath away from kissing her, it slips into the territory of the unconscious, as automatic as my heartbeat or blood rushing through my veins.

The Devil lies, even to himself.

But I can't lie to her. Not anymore. And if I sign her death warrant with my confession, well, it won't be the first time I've stormed Heaven to take back what's rightfully mine.

"I lied to you. About the prophecy." We've returned to the beginning, back to that first night when her powers spiraled out of control, and she begged me to ground her. Only now it's me who is off balance.

My hands curl around her back, drawing her flush against me, and I hear her breath catch. My lips brush hers, just the barest touch, and the tension drains from her body. She swallows a sound that could be a sob or a laugh or something in between.

I deepen the kiss, and her hands find their way around my back, fingertips digging into my shoulder blades as she unconsciously searches for my wings.

She tastes like light, and I've been in the darkness for so long.

I draw back just enough to speak again. "The prophecy. It wasn't about stopping Michael or Uriel." I push her against the altar, kissing my way down the column of her neck. I brush aside the strap of her dress, the black fabric the only thing keeping me from her skin. I kiss the bared flesh.

"It was a sacrifice." My movements still, and I look up, meeting Grace's eyes for the first time. "Your sacrifice."

Her face softens as understanding dawns on her, but instead of looking afraid for herself her grip merely tightens, pulling me impossibly closer. "I won't have you die for me," I say with a surety I want to believe I can guarantee.

"Then I won't," she replies, and we both heard the lie.

I kiss her again, her lips warm and pliant against mine, and I wonder, not for the first time if the inferno I feel when our skin connects is some remnant of Hell scorched into my DNA. Or if she's bringing the memory of the Lightbringer to the surface after he's been buried for so long in the shadows.

She pulls back, and I follow, trying to reclaim her mouth, but she presses one slender finger against my lips. "Don't try to save me again." I ignore her words and lift her up to sit on the edge of the altar, raising her height closer to my own.

"Lucifer." Her tone forces my reply.

"I can't promise you that, Grace. I *won't* promise you that." I pause before speaking again, feeling like a supplicant standing in this derelict church begging for understanding from this pitiless creature in a black sundress. "Don't ask that of me."

For an instant she looks ready to protest before nodding in agreement, accepting the stalemate. "I love you, you know." Her soft voice still seems to echo in the church, and I almost stagger under the weight of those pure, human words. "I don't expect anything from you. I don't even expect to survive this, but I needed you to know." The soft grey of her eyes hardens to steel as she reaches out to me, twining her fingers through mine. "Maybe all this pain, this trail of broken lives can *mean* something."

I press my lips to hers, silencing her words of a meaningful death. Every person who martyrs themselves for some worthy cause still dies, and there is never any meaning in that.

Instead, I push her down on the altar, her body arching upward to press against mine as the cool stone touches her back. Once I would have been laughing inside at this, taunting my Father with the prospect of defiling His house with one of these flawed creations.

How things have changed.

I hear a low moan as our mouths touch, and I don't know if it comes from my throat or hers. Around us, the room buzzes, the weight of her words pressing against me to the point that even drawing air into my lungs becomes a challenge. I'm drowning on dry land.

One hand comes up to cup the back of her head, shielding it from the unyielding stone, the only protection she seems willing to afford me right now. The kiss deepens, turning from something light and cautious as we relearn each other and the changes these revelations have wrought into something fierce and sudden as a hurricane.

In that moment, I understand why storms are named for people.

I am the Devil. The Fallen One. As unyielding as the tides, as unforgiving as nature. But in that moment, I feel the landscapes shifting as she carves new fault lines and fissures, reducing my walls to ashes and rubble.

And to think, when I met her, I was the one searching for cracks.

"Lucifer."

She sits up, resting on her elbows and watching me with a confidence that leaves me stunned. Every day she sheds a bit more of the fear that holds her back, the remnants of her old self crumbling away. If we survive this, Heaven will tremble at what she'll become.

If we survive this.

Her knees rest on either side of my legs, her skirt rucked up to her hips and it should look profane. She tamed her hair into a tight braid, and I take the end of it between my fingers, snapping the thin tie and carding my fingers through her liberated curls.

"You're obsessed with my hair."

"Utterly," I agree, twisting one lock for a moment before trailing my fingertips down the curve of her neck and shoulder. When I encounter the strap of her dress this time, I push it off and let my meandering hands cup her bared breast, brushing my thumb across the nipple until it tightens and her breath hitches.

"Lucifer."

I hear the impatience in her voice, but this very well could be it. If this is the last time, I have no intention of rushing. Every touch, every movement is with the intent of learning every cell and atom of her, branding myself into her muscle and sinew.

On this altar, I am devotion.

I wonder if Heaven is watching and what they think of their fallen brother now.

Grace has long since passed the point of laying back and allowing herself to be taken. She sits up fully, pushing me back onto my knees, and her fingers make quick work of my buttons, tugging the shirt-tails out of my pants. Her face is half in shadow, the high dusty windows of the church casting the room in murky light. With my shirt out of the way, Grace's fingers drift lower, tracing the muscles of my stomach to pause at my belt.

"This isn't goodbye," she says with vehemence. "This isn't one last time before we go off to war."

Her thoughts and past are still the pure white wall of nothingness they've always been, but under it all, I sense her absolute belief that *we are going to win*. We've both suffered enough, paid our dues to Heaven a thousand times over, and still come up short. Heaven has robbed us of so much. Heaven isn't taking this.

I haul Grace onto my lap, shifting back onto my heels, the unforgiving stone digging into my knees. She straddles me, and I use the moment to find my way under her skirt, eager to divest her of whatever lacy creation she's wearing.

She moves in for another kiss, wriggling against me, our bodies already aligned oh so perfectly except for the layers of fabric separating us.

For all my fondness for Italian suits, moments like this make me miss the robes.

She catches my bottom lip between her teeth, her fingers resting in the hair at the nape of my neck, and I ease her back down. When her back touches the stone this time, her hands fly to my belt again, steady and sure, all remnants of shyness forgotten. I peel off the bit of lace that had hinders me, gasping as her hand wraps around my length. I spread her knees with my own, and she pulls me closer without another word, drawing me up and into her.

I shift my weight, bracing myself on my elbows just enough to avoid crushing her. Beneath me, Grace looks shattered, a look no doubt mirrored on my own face. She pushes against me, her hips rocking upward, taking me in to the hilt. In sharp contrast to every frenzied coupling we've shared, I feel oddly restrained. In all likelihood, the world is burning to cinders outside the doors, my insane brother doing his best to bring the Hell he so despises to Earth.

But for now, I don't care about anything beyond heat and

friction, the slow, deliberate snap of my hips as I drive into her, and the ten points of pressure as she claws my back beneath my shirt.

I bury my face in her neck, the curtain of her hair falling around me, and I mouth the hollow of her throat, breathing in her scent. She sighs my name, and it sounds like a prayer on her lips, and I'm selfishly grateful for the curse that followed her family and lead her here. To me.

She rolls her hips, the slick slide as we fit together speeding up, the slow savor forgotten as need takes over. I feel her coming apart, feel both of our broken edges being ground down by this. Her tremors surround me, and she arches up as her release twists and coils through her, her cries of pleasure echoing off the bare walls of the church. I lose myself a moment later, my forehead resting against hers as shudders run through me from head to toe.

Quiet but for our ragged breaths, we are still. Grace presses her lips against my hair, her soft fingers tracing the length of my spine. I know I should pull myself together, but I cling to our sanctuary, however temporary it might be. Finally, I roll off her, straightening my clothes and letting myself enjoy an appreciative glance as Grace rights her own.

She slides off the altar, her shoes making the barest click on the stone floor, but beyond getting to her feet, she makes no move to leave the circle of my arms. I allow myself this last indulgence, allow the emotions I discarded long ago to swell in me as she tucks her head under my chin, her messy curls tickling my nose.

It isn't just affection, ease, or the need to protect. Not anymore.

I love her, with the same consecration I once felt in Heaven.

I only hope she can forgive me for what I'm about to do.

"Let's take a few moments to regroup," I murmur, my eyes

focusing on the heavy wooden door tucked away at the edge of the nave. An open padlock hangs down, the metal dull and corroded with dust. "I think that might be an office. If it's all the same to you, I'd rather not sit on a pew during our war council." I keep my tone flat, almost bored.

Grace giggles, the carefree sound reminding me with screeching certainty just how young she is.

This is the only way.

The walk across the church floor is short, but every step seems to echo with finality. I open the door and peer inside, seeing a heavy wooden desk too large and cumbersome for the priest to bother bringing to his next parish. Other random detritus of the church lays scattered around the small room – a broken candlestick, the cheap metal not worth the effort of melting down to scrap, two high-backed chairs stacked with musty smelling bibles, a cracked mirror hanging on the back wall. The only window is scarcely larger than a sheet of paper and coated with a thick layer of greasy dust.

"Homey," Grace says, disdainfully. As she moves past me into the room, I grab her waist, pulling her back that final foot of space between us and capturing her lips with my own. Her head tilts upward, and she rises on her toes, her mouth opening under mine, stealing my breath. Or I steal hers. At this point, I've long since lost the ability to tell.

She breaks the kiss first, pulling back just enough to speak, our foreheads touching. She smiles, and it's like the sun coming out from a cloud, and I almost falter.

"What was that for?" she asks, a teasing edge to her voice that speaks of comfort, of familiarity, and I draw my resolve into myself.

"Whatever happens, this was real." I tuck a strand of her hair behind her ear, my voice wavering the slightest bit. "You made the Devil love you. Remember that."

A look of alarm crosses her face an instant before I shove

her through the door, slamming the heavy oak and fastening the padlock, trapping her inside.

The thick glass of the tiny porthole window on the door distorts her features, but I see the betrayal and shock clear as day.

"Don't do this, Lucifer!" she pleads, pounding on the door.

I feel her trying to gather her scattered emotions through the bond, and I rest my hand against the doorjamb, calling up the memory of Hellfire and the blistering heat. The metal grows hotter under my touch, the molten steel of the frame binding with the decorative brass edges of the door, sealing her in.

Grace will be able to break it eventually, but it'll buy me the time I need.

"You don't need to protect me, Lucifer. I can help you stop him!"

I shake my head before speaking. "Even if we win, Grace, there are consequences to killing an angel. Consequences that will leave your soul in tatters." Her hand rests on the glass as she watches me, her wide eyes pleading me to reconsider. "There are some things Heaven doesn't forgive, no matter what your bloodline might be."

I turn and walk away to the sound of Grace pounding on the door and screaming my name.

❦ 20 ❧

GRACE

For the second time, I watch Lucifer walk away from me.

I thought nothing could hurt more than seeing any affection he had for me wither. I was so wrong.

I faintly hear the slam of the main church doors as they close behind him, leaving me alone. I yank on the door handle ineffectually, trying to summon up the strength that threw Michael across a mausoleum and drove Uriel to his knees, but nothing.

Silence.

Every step takes him closer to Uriel. To a fight he already expects to lose. I slap the heel of my hand against the door, barely holding back the urge to sob.

It isn't going to end like this.

I sit down on the dusty floor, pulling my knees up to my chest as I scan the room, hoping a secret door or an escape hatch might suddenly reveal itself. Instead, it's still just a room filled with the abandoned church's leftovers, junk too worthless to bother moving.

Pressing my forehead against my knees, I do something I haven't done since I was a child.

I pray.

"I don't really know how this goes," I say, my voice thick with the tears I've finally given up holding back. "I've never exactly been the praying type, but God or any angels listening that aren't complete psychos. . . don't let him die." My voice sounds so small, my words swallowed up as I sit huddled on the floor. I lift my head, staring at the dirty window and the murky daylight that filters through the dust. "He made mistakes, but I think he paid for them long enough."

Anger flares in me, and I stand up, taking a step closer to the window. "And what exactly was I paying for? What was my mother paying for?"

"Oh, Gracie."

I whirl around at the voice, that achingly familiar sound I've dreamed of hearing for seven years, but I see nothing.

I shake my head at myself, grabbing the broken candlestick from the desk and turning back to the window and my diatribe. I slam the candlestick against the window, the thick glass splintering under the blow. I don't harbor any illusions of fitting through the tiny opening, but the destruction brings me the tiniest bit of focus.

"Grace, you're so strong now. So close to what you need to be."

I turn quickly enough this time to catch movement in the mirror. I cross the room to stand in front of it within a second, my hands shaking as I brush away a few cobwebs.

It should be a reflection of myself distorted from the cracked glass, but it isn't. It takes my brain a moment to catch up with what I'm seeing before I can speak.

"Mom?"

She nods, the edges of her body looking hazy like I'm seeing her through a fogged up window.

"We don't have much time, Grace. Neither of you has much time." I press my fingertips against the glass, feeling the fractured edges bite into my skin.

"Mom," I repeat, trying to memorize everything about her – the same messy curls I inherited, the scar across her left eyebrow from falling out of a tree when she was thirteen, the flowered hippie top she'd been wearing the day she died.

She smiles, the sad, wistful smile I remember, frozen in time in the photographs scattered around my house. "Do you know what you did, Grace? You made the Devil feel. You carried the Lightbringer out of darkness." She presses her fingers against mine from the other side of the glass, and I can almost feel her. "And he brought you back too. You just need to remember who you are. Who you came from." My mother stares at me from the other side of the glass and a million miles away, her lips set in a grim line. "This city, this world? It's not theirs anymore. Any parent understands that. One day you have to let your children stand on their own two feet."

"I miss you, Mom," I whisper. Prophecies and epic battles forgotten, at least for the moment.

"We miss you too, sweetie. But you're needed here." She smiles the same mischievous grin usually reserved for my father. "I like him, by the way." She looks toward the door, and my gaze lands on the walls penning me in here. "You could always open the door, Grace. You just need to remember how."

When I look back at the mirror, only my own refection in the dusty glass greets me.

I walk to the door and put my hands on the knob, turning with all my strength.

It doesn't budge.

"Nothing worth anything ever comes easy," I mutter.

. . .

I WAS twelve or thirteen and sick with the worst case of the flu I'd had in my life, the world burning with the red haze of a fever dream as I drifted in and out of awareness. My mother curled up in bed with me, sponging my forehead with a wet washcloth smelling of peppermint and the soft honey scent of meadowsweet.

"I've never told you the story of our family. Of who the Celestin women are. Of why I kept my name." She tossed the washcloth back into the fragrant water, brushing my sweaty hair away from my forehead.

My eyes slipped shut for a moment before opening again, and my glassy stare saw my mother who always seemed so powerful looking subdued and alone. "Secrets are hard when you can't share them. I know you won't remember hearing this, Grace, but I'll remember telling you." She leaned forward, her lips close to my ear and her arms around me, her presence grounding me. "You're special. You're going to save the world one day, all on your own. I wish I could be there that day to see it."

I coughed, whimpering as the shudders wracked my body, and my Mom squeezed me tighter. "It's going to be hard. It's going to hurt so much you'll want to lock yourself away, but nothing worth anything ever comes easy. You're going to do it, Grace, and wherever I am, I'll be watching."

A TEAR ROLLS down my cheek, and I wipe it away, wondering where that memory came from and if it's even real. I'd been wretchedly sick, coming in and out of awareness for a day while my body rode out the worse of the illness, and my mother had sat by my side the entire time, bathing my forehead with one of the many herbal concoctions she brewed to bring down my fever.

I remember her singing softly, snippets of Led Zeppelin and the Allman Brothers flowing over me, the constant murmur of her voice comforting me as I rode the waves of the fever.

But I never remembered her words, the halting story staying locked away in the recesses of my mind for a decade. I wonder if Erzulie handed the story of my future to my mother along with one of her mojo bags or if it was something she had read in the cards she kept hidden in her bedside table.

The hows and the whys don't matter much anymore. Nothing matters except for that door.

But the women in my family haven't just been delicate creatures who laid back and let fate take them. They carved their way with blood and fire and bone. The memories flooding me aren't my own, but they are my legacy.

That fire in 1921? Arelia set it, letting the blaze take her to buy her husband enough time to spirit Genevieve away.

Genevieve drowned because Uriel rammed his sword through the floor of the boat she was escaping in. She dove into the Mississippi, forcing Uriel to follow while her family swam to shore and ran.

Rose wore her heart too open and trusted too easily, but when Erzulie crossed her path, she trusted the right person. Even in the asylum, she never gave up. Even with her dying breath, she wove the protections Erzulie had taught her around Serafine.

Serafine, wild, rambling Serafine who traveled West but still came back when the Crescent City called. She was the first to live long enough to see her granddaughter born. She nearly took Uriel with her that day, binding him with blood magics that took a decade for him to tear through.

And Marianne. Battered and broken with her arterial blood draining away and she still beat back an Archangel with white-hot fire and twisted metal.

The Celestin women? We aren't cursed.

We're warriors.

The line stretches back through the centuries, through unnumbered cities and continents, names lost but never forgotten. With the power of every one of them boiling in me, I press my hand against the door.

And I push.

❧ 21 ❦

LUCIFER

I feel the finality ringing in every step of the short walk to The Saint, every block bringing me closer to finishing this and slaying another of my brothers.

I ended so many of them during the war, all lower level seraphim that both sides fed to each other, nothing more than angelic cannon fodder. I didn't even know most of their names and have long forgotten nearly all of their faces. It was war, and in war, there were always deaths.

But this- this is unneeded.

The hotel sits empty, a lone police car waiting half a block away, all the city could spare when riots are breaking out on every street. The two rookie officers that drew the short straw and ended up here make no move to exit their car. I can't say I blame them.

A few hotel patrons linger in the street, waiting for cabs that won't show or the black-eyed valet. He took a stolen Tesla for a joyride and drove it into the levee, so they aren't leaving anytime soon. The crowd of possessed that surrounds the entrance blocks them from any hope of returning to their hotel, so they stand frozen, staring at their phones in Sisyphean denial of the entire situation.

I push through the mob, the possessed souls having enough foresight in their lizard brains to recognize the Lord of Hell in their midst. For all that they're enjoying their spring break revels, they all know exactly where they're destined to end up and that it won't do well to cross me.

I kick open the door hard enough to crack the glass.

"Uriel!" I bellow, my voice reverberating off the empty lobby.

My brother peers over the railing on the second floor, surveying the chaos in the street with a detached air that infuriates me. Uriel vaults over the edge, dropping down with a force that splinters the front desk under his feet.

"Lightbringer," he says, barely sparing me a glance as his eyes dart around the room searching, no doubt, for Grace. "I'm not interested in killing you right now. Where is the Last?"

I ignore his question. "You had your Garden, Uriel. What gives you the right to unleash this on the world? Is this some childish cry for attention? If our Father hasn't shown up for your other exploits, he's not likely to make an appearance now!"

Uriel springs on me with a ferocity of a wild animal, teeth bared in a crazed smile that would look far more at home in Hell than in Heaven. He shifts his wrist, his blade sliding into his hand with an ease for violence that looks all too familiar.

He moves like a viper, slashing out and feinting back so quickly I don't feel the first slash across my chest until the burn of the Heaven-forged metal sets in. This isn't the Uriel I remember, escaping to Eden as the wars raged outside the gates, turning his back on both sides in favor of picking flowers in his own private sanctuary.

I wonder what drove him to this.

Then I remember I don't care.

I grab the front of Uriel's robes, yanking him close enough to render both our weapons useless as I grapple for his sword. I lose my grip on my blade, and I hear the clatter of metal on the tile beneath our feet as I launch him at the bar. Uriel spreads his wings in an effort to stop the momentum to no avail. He hits the mirrored wall, the glass no match for his bulk. Dozens of bottles of liquor shatter, filling the room with the sharp scent of the spilled alcohol.

I stalk across the lobby, pausing to grab my sword from the ground. Uriel lays slumped behind the bar, top-shelf booze soaking into his clothing, but I know there's no chance that our little tussle was enough to knock him out, let alone seriously injure him.

"Get up," I snarl, "I'll at least give you the dignity of dying on your feet."

Uriel springs to life, jamming his sword into my thigh with a force that drives me to my knees. One of his hands closes around my throat, dragging me back to my feet as he twists the blade. I stay silent, the searing agony ripping through my leg bringing the clarity only pain can provide.

"It's been too long since anyone challenged you, brother," Uriel sneers. "You've gone soft."

In my peripheral vision, I see Phenex stagger in, barely supported by Michael, the entire left side of his suit red with blood, and I'm amazed that he's even managing to stay upright. Michael appears to have fared better, though he watches Uriel with a wariness that makes me certain they fought as well.

The momentary distraction is enough to make Uriel take his eyes off me. Dropping my blade, I shove myself backward, the razor edge ripping through the flesh of my upper thigh, and I silently thank the torment of eons in Hell as only a low moan escapes me as the divine sword burns my flesh like acid.

I limp back weaponless, trying to put distance between myself and Uriel as I plot my next move.

Phenex elbows Michael away, moving toward me, but Michael's words ring out.

"All of Heaven is watching the choice you make right now, Phenex. Choose wisely."

He hesitates for just a moment before shaking his head, continuing his advance until he's just beyond the striking distance of Uriel.

Phenex was never a warrior. He fights when he has no other choice and his back is to the wall, but he never revels in the sounds of breaking bones and rending flesh. The Hell-forged daggers hidden in his boots haven't seen use in centuries, but Phenex still plucks them from their hiding spot and has one embedded in Uriel's shoulder to the hilt before I can blink. He tosses me the second dagger, and I catch it easily.

I see Uriel move, and I open my mouth to warn Phenex too late. In an instant, he has Phenex by his pale hair, wrenching his head back to bare his throat. "I thought you'd be smart enough to slink back to Hell. You always did pick the wrong side, Phenex."

The cut he makes is deep, not enough to kill instantly, but enough to send Phenex to his knees, his hands ineffectually trying to stop the torrent of blood.

🧩 22 🧩

GRACE

I run.

The Saint is only a few blocks away, but every step feels like running in a dream. My limbs feel too slow, as if gravity itself is trying to hold me back, but I shrug it off. When I turn the corner onto Canal Street, the mob surrounding the hotel is thicker than Mardi Gras as hundreds of damned souls watch Heaven and Hell battle it out inside a hotel lobby.

They part as I grow closer, clearing a path to the door. The power spirals through my veins, burning so much brighter than it had that very first night. The memory of those moments feels detached like watching a movie of another person's life, that terrified girl crawling the walls, begging for respite long gone.

This time though, the fear never comes. Lucifer's pain echoes through the bond, and the piercing intensity of it would have broken me even a day ago. But buried in all the noise of his existence, hidden below the screaming crescendo of anger and defiance is a deep well of iron resolve.

He believes.

He believes that stopping Uriel and protecting me is worth it, even if it costs him his life. It may have taken thousands of years, but the Devil finally sees humanity as something worth saving.

But revelation or not, I'm not going to let anyone else decide the destiny for one more Celestin woman. After all, I'm the Last, and I know with absolute certainty what is going to happen.

The princess is going to save herself in this one.

My fingers scarcely brush the handle, and the door springs open, shards of the already cracked glass clinking softly as they fall to the floor when the door strikes the back wall.

In an instant, I take in the destruction around me – the splintered mound of lacquered wood that was once the front desk, the rubble half the bar has been reduced to, Phenex face down on the floor in a pool of his own blood.

I crouch down next to him, feeling the defiant spark of his soul still clinging to life when I touch his shoulder.

A few feet away, Michael stands as a mute sentry to the scene. When I rise, he takes a step forward, his intent to stop me written plainly across his face.

"No," I say, the finality of the word stopping Michael in his tracks.

Lucifer's head snaps up when he hears my voice, his dark eyes meeting mine from across the room, and in a flash, it all falls away. I see beyond the brief glimpse he gave me of his true face - the exquisite majesty of an Archangel, once the most beautiful of *all* the Archangels, scorched black and twisted with thousands of years of darkness and hatred and pain. Even hidden under all that, I see the glow of the Lightbringer. His favorite. The Morningstar. In the space of a second, I see what he was and what he's becoming again, and it's so beautiful.

Until his face contorts in a grimace of pain as Uriel slams his sword into his back, piercing his heart.

Lucifer drops to his knees, his hand uselessly clutching where the blade protrudes from his chest. Uriel pulls the sword from his body with a sick sucking sound that fades into silence.

I don't notice the noise of Lucifer's knife clattering on the floor or Uriel's gloating voice rambling on about cleansing the world. The sirens and car alarms in the distance wither to nothing in my ears. It all fades into the sound of my heartbeat as I take those last few steps to Lucifer, my hands catching him as he pitches forward. I roll him onto his back, and his eyes meet mine. Bit by bit the life ebbs out of them, quicker and quicker with each breath. His fingers, slick with blood, twist through mine.

I bow my head, trying to remember how to breathe.

I thought we would win.

We were supposed to win.

"Choose."

I lift my head to see Lucifer's eyes slip closed, and the voice speaks again. "Choose."

It sounds like my mother. My father. Erzulie. Talia. A dozen female voices I don't recognize that can only be my ancestors.

And underneath them all is Lucifer.

Everyone who ever touched my life, all speaking over each other until they melt into one voice.

"Choose. Heaven or Hell. Light or dark. Good or evil. You must choose."

I place my left hand over the exit wound in the center of Lucifer's chest, the blood welling from it staining my fingers a deep crimson. My right hand still clenches Lucifer's, his grip stronger than a dying man's should be. I don't look away from his face when I speak, my words intended only for him. "I choose both. I choose neither."

With the last drop of strength in his body, Lucifer presses the blood-slick knife into my palm. My fingers close around it, and I whirl upward, ramming it into Uriel's throat to the hilt, the Hell-forged knife going deep enough to sever his spinal cord. In the half-second before his existence is snuffed out, the angel's eyes meet mine with disbelief. I lean close to his face and whisper, "I choose him."

Blinding light fills the room as Uriel expires, the last flare of a dying star. A week ago, my mortal eyes would have been boiled in their sockets, but today I simply turn away, forgetting his cruel existence before his body hits the floor.

Lucifer struggles to his feet, his fingers shaking slightly as he presses them through the tear in his shirt to touch the unmarred skin. Behind me, I heard Michael's sharp intake of breath as Phenex sits up.

"Grace," he murmurs, words finally failing him. Lucifer's true face recedes into the background, hidden under the façade he shows the world. The look of awe on his features makes me wonder just what he sees now when he looks at me. He starts to reach out to me, his fingers spread, before clenching his hand and drawing his arm back. He closes his eyes, taking a deep breath to steady himself before looking past me to where the others stand.

Michael rounds the bar, broken glass crunching under his feet. He openly stares at both of us with a reverence that does nothing but amuse Lucifer.

"Would you like to take a picture, brother?" The snide comment breaks the tension, and even Michael chuckles. Resurrection certainly hasn't changed that aspect of Lucifer.

"I should return to Heaven," Michael says, looking at Uriel's body with unexpected regret.

"Agreed," Lucifer replies, the brief levity sobering. "Let his garrison know his fate, lest any of them have any ideas of following in his footsteps. It's over."

Michael nods, and an instant later he's gone, taking Uriel's body with him. If I was expecting a brotherly reconciliation, I was certainly mistaken.

The scrape of wood on the tile floor as he rights a barstool brings our attention back to Phenex. Ducking behind the bar, he grabs the first unbroken bottle his fingers touch, popping the lid off and taking a deep drink of the clear liquor before slumping down on the barstool.

Grimacing at the taste he mutters, "Warm vodka, lovely" before taking another swig. "Beggars can't be choosers." He offers the bottle to Lucifer. Lucifer stares at him silently, far longer than is comfortable, and Phenex shrinks back into himself. Finally relenting, Lucifer grabs the bottle and drinks before passing it to me and flipping over two more chairs.

I wince at the flavorless burn but don't comment, watching as Lucifer sits next to Phenex. "I know why you did it," Lucifer says, resting his hands against the lacquered surface of the bar. "You don't belong in Hell. You never did." Lucifer reaches across the space between them and clasps Phenex's shoulder for a moment. "Don't return to Hell. The way will be barred to you." Lucifer takes the bottle from me, taking another long drink before passing it to Phenex without looking.

"I can't undo bringing you into this all those years ago. And promise or no, Michael can't let you back into Heaven." Lucifer twists on the barstool, leaning back and staring out the wall of windows at the crowd still milling outside. "But I think this world is big enough that you can find your place in it." Lucifer glances over at me, a small smile crossing his lips. "Maybe we both can."

The Devil, a fallen angel, and. . . whatever the Hell I am

sit in a destroyed bar as evening bleeds into night. There's a joke in there somewhere.

The whole city wakes up from its daze. The wailing sirens grow louder as police and ambulances tear down the streets, the barely controlled chaos that stands for order in New Orleans finally reasserting itself.

The trapped souls were cast down to Hell at the moment of Uriel's death, but the sudden freedom won't heal all the scars. Phenex hangs a few steps behind us, the dried blood across this throat doing little to conceal the ragged scar there. Somehow I pulled him back from death, but he'll wear the scars from Uriel's weapons for the rest of his existence.

Despite the size of the crowd, silence falls across the street again. The bewildered citizens wander down the street, searching for their cars or their homes, picking at the blank spaces of time inside their heads like a wound. So many of them are already Hellbound because of Uriel's interference.

But then I see Lucifer, gazing up at the stars from the middle of the street like he's seeing them for the first time.

It never is too late for a second chance.

Once I would have hesitated on the sidelines, waiting and wishing for things to be different. For so many years, life just happened to me, but as I watch Lucifer look at me, beckoning me to his side with the wicked grin I know so well, I realize that I earned this.

I spent seven years locked in guilt for surviving if I allowed myself to feel anything at all. I forged our future in trials and blood.

Erzulie was right when she said, *"You both might just save each other."*

My name is Grace Celestin, and I don't quite know what I am anymore. As I take Lucifer's hand I think, *that makes two of us.*

———————

I DREAMED of wings for so long.

Even after everything I've seen and done in the last few days, I can't help gasping when I see them. The brief glimpses in the past can't compare.

From tip to tip they span a dozen feet, the flight feathers as long as my arm. Under the harsh fluorescence of the street-lights, they glow smoky grey, the color of smooth worn stone, of ashes.

Not black. Not anymore.

"Can I?" I leave the question dangling in the air, sensing what I'm asking for is an intimacy that goes far beyond anything we've shared. Lucifer inclines his head forward, just the barest hint of movement.

Around us, the streets have emptied, the formerly possessed having dragged themselves away from The Saint at record speeds. Michael is long gone, and Phenex has slipped away as well to lick his wounds and consider his future.

Lucifer stands stock still, the light breeze ruffling his feathers. He looks stunned, as though he hasn't quite finished processing what has happened.

I take the last few steps to reach him. Up close, the wings are startlingly beautiful, and I feel the first inkling of under-standing Heaven. Tentatively I run my fingers through the feathers, marveling at the cloud-softness of the shorter feath-ers, feeling the powerful muscle and bone beneath them.

The noise that escapes his throat is almost a purr as he leans back into my touch. Lucifer's eyes fall shut, and his face relaxes into a look of pure *contentment*. Some tiny part of me had wondered if the bond between us was something tempo-rary that would dissipate into nothing once the battles were fought and won.

Those thoughts crumble to dust as his wings wrap around

me, cocooning me in warm feathers that smell charged, like the air before a lightning strike. Already off balance when he crushes his mouth to mine, I wrap my arms around his neck. I feel the pressure of his wings against my back, holding me up, and I know he'll never allow me to fall.

His mouth opens under mine, and I taste the tang of blood from his split lip, long since healed. One of his hands creeps across my waist before tucking under my knees and lifting me up.

And suddenly we're airborne.

Lucifer's wings beat quietly, the flight feathers cutting through the air and carrying us higher and higher. Below us, the city rushes by, a blur of lights. The air grows thin and cool, dizzying and exhilarating all at once. I bury my face in his shirt, still stiff with dried blood, the rip in the fabric reminding me of how close I came to losing him.

I healed him. I think we healed each other.

After so many years lost and alone, I feel *sure* for the first time. What I am now, what the future holds, those soul-tearing consequences of killing an angel - I have more questions than answers. Until I look at him and I know with the certainty of breathing that the choices I made were the right ones.

Soaring above the city in the Devil's arms, I finally know where I belong.

23

LUCIFER

We return to her house, where it truly began.

The sky is just beginning to lighten with the promise of dawn when I land on the steps leading to her door. Grace stumbles ever so slightly before regaining her footing. The ginger cat still naps on the porch. When we pass, he opens one green eye to stare, still looking deeply unimpressed with us both.

The front door creaks open with the lightest touch, the pieces of the shattered lock rattling around inside the worn brass knob. We scarcely notice the wreckage Phenex and Uriel left in the house, skirting past a demolished coffee table, broken glass tacky with drying blood crunching under our feet.

The coming days will be filled with discovery as I learn the tiniest facets of her life and let her see beyond the screen of the Devil into Lucifer. The idea of getting to know each other without the threat of imminent destruction is new, to say the least. All I know is that I want her. In my bed. By my side. As an equal for as long as she'll have me.

Grace presses her hand against my chest, the softness of

her palm a contrast to the stiffness of the blood-soaked fabric of my ruined shirt. The noise of ripping cloth sounds loud in the silent house as her fingers poke through the tear in the shirt and pull. I stand still, letting her claw at the already tattered fabric until it hangs open. She pushes it off my shoulders, letting it fall at our feet.

The momentary frenzy passed, Grace's hand is back on my chest, the slightest tremor going through her fingers as she traces them over my heart where the ugly wound would have been.

My voice is barely above a whisper when I speak. "You saved the Devil's life. Some might say that was the wrong choice."

Grace stays quiet, her eyes affixed to the spot on my chest that she healed. A hundred quips about being in her debt and at her mercy spring to my mind, borne of a lifetime where favors and servitude are two sides of the same coin. I hold my tongue, letting her gather her thoughts without interruption.

When she speaks, her voice is as soft as my own, the weight of her choice and her actions already felt through Heaven and Hell with the force of an earthquake. Now, when everything is quiet, these words are only for us.

"It was worth it." She looks up at me, reminding me just how small she is. The top of her head barely reaches my shoulders. To my unasked question, she replies, "Sacrificing Heaven."

I tense, the old hatred at my Father threatening to boil over that someone so *good* would have the gates barred to her. "I never wanted that for you." If she hears the catch in my voice, she doesn't comment.

We called Michael God's Poison behind his back and to his face, but that nickname ended up with the wrong angel.

She takes my face in her hands, and I catch the first glimpse of the carefree girl she once was. Battered and bloody, surrounded by the wreckage of her home and lost family, she looks happy.

She looks free.

She takes a step back, and I follow into her bedroom, drawn to her with the same immutable want I've felt since I first touched her in the square.

This girl. This powerful, eternal, but still so human girl with the blood of Heaven in her veins and the blood of two Archangels on her hands takes the Devil to her bed.

If Heaven and Hell are watching, they keep silent for once.

The worlds of angels and devils, the damned and the forgiven, all blur a bit more at our union, black and white fading into smoke grey as the feathers beneath her fingertips.

I told her once that the Devil doesn't come dressed in horns and a red cape. He comes in the guise of all you've ever wanted.

I wanted vengeance and amusement. My brother's head on a stick and the chance to drown myself in this flesh-filled world and forget.

To most of the world, I am still called many things.

Prince of Lies. Lord of Hell. The Supreme Tempter of Mankind. I am not so naïve to expect humanity to find a new scapegoat for their sins anytime soon.

When I Fell, my light was snuffed out. I embraced the blackness, telling myself I reveled in the torture and the screams, and a lie spoken often enough has a way of bleeding into truth. But ever so slowly the bits of me lost to the darkness have crept back, and I can already feel the awakening of the Lightbringer. The Morningstar.

Not *His* favorite. Not anymore.

With her by my side, I'm something different. Something better.

I am not what I was.

ACKNOWLEDGMENTS

To Joe - Thank you for putting up with my unrelenting obsession with making this novel into everything I hoped it would be. I love you.

***

To Tarin - Thank you for always being my sounding board, and for the endless FaceTime calls where you let me play out conversations with my characters.

***

To Aaron - Thank you for not thinking I was crazy when I called you from a grocery store in North Carolina to exclaim over my idea of writing a romance novel about the Devil.

***

And most of all, thank you to my readers. This book started

from a random idea I had over a year ago and grew into so much more. I hope you enjoyed reading it as much as I enjoyed writing it!

Ava

ABOUT THE AUTHOR

Ava Martell was born on Friday the 13th, but she always believed in making her own luck and writing her own story. She is a firm believer that love really does conquer all, but sometimes you have to take the long way around to get there.

She lives in Austin, Texas with her husband, German Shepherd, and two deeply spoiled cats. Ava loves a good gin and tonic to wind her down or wind her up, depending on the occasion, and the only thing better than a good cocktail is a good story.

If you enjoyed this book, and want to receive information on any new books, sign up for Ava's mailing list here.

Follow Ava on social media

Facebook
Twitter
Tumblr
Instagram

Official site
avamartell.com

msavamartell@gmail.com

First Man

Throw out the rules.

Let the sparks fly.

And pray for a happily ever after. . .

Adam Edwards drifts in the wide world, searching for his next
adventure. When his journey around the globe brings him to
America he finds a love he never expects and a loss he can't endure.

Ember Pierson is 18 and counting down the days until graduation
frees her from small town life. Everything changes when Adam rolls
into town and takes a job teaching high school English, and Ember
hatches a plan. . .

CPSIA information can be obtained
at www.ICGtesting.com
Printed in the USA
FSHW012034110520
70159FS